IS THIS WHAT YOU WANT?

IS THIS WHAT YOU WANT?

The Asham Award Short-Story Collection

Edited by Kate Pullinger

BLOOMSBURY

Bloomsbury Publishing Plc, 36 Soho Square, London W1D 3QY

A CIP catalogue record for this book is available from the British Library

ISBN 978 0 7475 8712 5

10 9 8 7 6 5 4 3 2

Typeset by Hewer Text UK Ltd, Edinburgh
Printed in Great Britain by Clays Ltd, St Ives plc

Bloomsbury Publishing, London, New York and Berlin

All papers used by Bloomsbury Publishing are natural,
recyclable products made from wood grown in well-managed
forests. The manufacturing processes conform to the
environmental regulations of the country of origin

www.bloomsbury.com/asham

www.ashamaward.com

CONTENTS

CAROLE BUCHAN

Foreword

Now into its second decade, the Asham Award maintains its commitment to women's writing. In this anthology, as always, we bring together unknown writers from across the country with some of our most prestigious and exciting established writers of short fiction. It is a heady mix and one which has played an important part in raising the status of the short story.

The Asham Award has a reputation for excellence and in this collection we believe we have raised the stakes even higher. Chair of judges Patricia Duncker, commenting on the twelve winning stories, said these were tales which 'moved, puzzled, gripped and entertained. And the very best merited re-reading at once.'

This Asham collection pushes at the boundaries, provokes, excites and is a remarkable example of the range of women's writing. The Award has developed a momentum of its own and each year the standard gets higher. The Asham Trust aims to support and encourage new writing and we are proud of the fact that many of our award winners have gone on to make names for themselves in the world of fiction. Last year, for example, one of our prizewinners from a previous competition, Naomi Alderman, won the Orange first fiction prize for her novel *Disobedience*.

The Asham Award encourages women to take what, in some cases, is the first tentative step on the ladder towards a career in writing. Each of the one hundred or so shortlisted writers receives a critique of their story in the first stage of the judging process. The final twelve work on a one-to-one basis with our editor Kate Pullinger to fine-tune their stories for publication. In addition, the Asham Trust runs workshops led by some of the many commissioned writers who have contributed to our anthologies over the past twelve years.

We believe we have helped hundreds of new writers to find their voice and the courage to let that voice be heard, even if they do not make it into the final.

The Asham Award owes a huge debt of gratitude to its judges Patricia Duncker, Antonia Byatt and Tobias Hill, who devoted much time and care to making their final choice and were often faced with difficult decisions.

In addition we are indebted to our commissioned writers, each of whom has made a great contribution to contemporary fiction in publishing today: Tessa Hadley, Nancy Lee, Emily Perkins and Rachel Cusk. They are joined by Patricia Duncker and Kate Pullinger, both of whom have supported the Asham Award since the beginning.

We are grateful to Bloomsbury Publishing for their invaluable support over the past three years, which has helped to elevate the status of the Asham Award, and to the John S. Cohen Foundation, the Arts Council, and East Sussex County Council, without whom this anthology could not have come about.

Carole Buchan,
Administrator, Asham Literary Endowment Trust,
Lewes, East Sussex

- *If you love short stories, look out for the short-story festival* – **Small Wonder** – *organised jointly by the Asham and Charleston Trusts, which takes place at Charleston, near Lewes, from 20 to 23 September 2007.*
- *For more information visit www.ashamaward.com or www.charleston.org.uk.*
- *Visit both sites for more information about other literature projects to be launched in the coming months.*

THE ASHAM AWARD WINNERS 2007

First prize   Marian Garvey for 'All That's Left'

Second prize   Lois McEwan for 'Mrs Laidlaw's Event Horizon'

Third prize   Janey Huber for 'The Serpent's Child'

The judges for the Asham Award 2007 are
Patricia Duncker, Antonia Byatt and Tobias Hill

The Asham Award is sponsored by
the Asham Literary Endowment Trust,
the John S. Cohen Foundation, the Arts Council
and East Sussex County Council

ANNA BRITTEN

The Girl from the Dotcom

I F HE did not sign the contract today, Emily Quinn reminded herself as she checked her teeth in a boulangerie window, she was for *le chop*. A goner. Dead.

She had never come face to face with the sack before. When others had malfunctioned or misconducted their sorry way to being frogmarched through the revolving doors, she'd always been the one waving sadly, holding the departed's still-warm coffee mug close to her chest. Now that she was on the brink of such shame herself, it was a strangely thrilling sensation. It reminded her of crouching, trembling, on the edge of Brockwell Lido as a child, waiting, longing, for her younger brother to shove her into the cold, fluorescent water. Like Peter Pan might have said if he'd ever been on a graduate employment scheme: to be fired would be an awfully big adventure.

But it wasn't going to happen today. Oh no. One stuffy, no-clue, Sunday-league, old-school French music publisher versus Progress. How much of a challenge could it be? Come on, Emily, she urged. There was a post-deal bottle of champagne with the team riding on this; the MD had given her a thousand machine-fresh francs to buy it. She had her Powerpoint presentation. A glossy brochure. The spiel. And her all-important English accent, the chief reason she was hired by the American-owned dotcom which had thrown so many francs at her she had been too embarrassed to say no, or even to ask if she could think it over. If she had told the MD she had, in fact, slunk over to Paris merely to waitress, paint and speak French – and think – he'd have laughed until his crisp, blue YSL shirt split open to reveal the 666 engraved on his chest. Then he'd have fixed her with his hungry, yellow eye and asked her why, then, had she replied so enthusiastically, so gushingly, to the advert? And she'd have had to reply that it was fear. Fear of being left behind. Behind was bad.

Number ten, Quai de Jemmapes teetered upwards from the lumpy, cobbled towpath of an oily canal, like a Duplo tower built on a rumpled rug. She buzzed 'Duliège' and immediately received a sharp buzz in reply. She heaved aside the cathedral-sized door and entered a dark, tiled hallway lined with mailboxes. 'Here,' called a deep, crumbly male voice from above her head. 'Ah. The girl from the dotcom.'

Bristling at his condescending tone, she ascended the staircase to see the white-crowned head of Marcel Duliège looming over her from the third-floor landing, gravity tugging his brown, jowly face into that of a bloated corpse. Except a bloated corpse wouldn't have been playing air piano on the banister to a recording of 'Windmills of Your Mind'.

Rictus grin in place, she cruised into executive mode. They shook hands. His was hot and damp. She accepted a glass of water (no Ricard, thank you, she had to go back to the office afterwards), and a seat on a rescued-from-the-rubble-of-Versailles style sofa covered in colourful woven cushions, with a studied blend of friendliness and frost.

Was he going to turn that music off? Right. First, the blind-him-with-science approach. In one smooth motion, she slid her laptop on to the coffee table, snapped open its lid and rotated it towards him. At the top of the screen was a cartoon drawing of a well-thumbed book, with a big red 'X' next to it. Beneath it, a printer and a big green tick. The monitor cast a faint blue light on Marcel Duliège's baggy features. With a slightly peeved expression, he let her deliver the speech which was supposed to look off the cuff but (as her bathroom mirror would attest) was anything but. He rubbed his upper lip, the bristles crunching under his knuckle, as she listed the reasons why he should hand over his little catalogue of songs, suites and soundtracks to a website that would digitise them and deliver them 'straight to the printers of musicians all over the world'. He took a gulp of Ricard as she pointed out what an unacceptable waste of time it was for a busy, modern person to walk to a sheet music store and purchase a whole set of songs when they could get the precise one they required off the internet 'in seconds'. At one point he tiptoed away to get more ice from the freezer as if he was sneaking out of a movie to pee. She followed him with her eyes there and back, refusing to be put off by this facade – it had to be a facade – of nonchalance.

At the end he said: 'But I like walking to sheet music stores.'

Emily nodded sympathetically. 'Oh.'

So. The peer pressure approach. She unsheathed a spreadsheet from the zip pocket of her computer case. To herself she read: 'Drafted letter to: "Editions Oiseau Bleu; EMI France; Jean Bouvier . . ."' Aloud she reported: 'Editions Oiseau Bleu; EMI France; Jean Bouvier; they've all either signed, or are signing this week. I'm sure they'd be more than happy to tell you why.' If he'd been a proper businessman, this would be a dangerous, foolhardy bluff.

3

Looking at him, though – a sixty- or even seventy-year-old man with a frayed cheesecloth shirt and a grog-blossomed nose – Emily was sure her feint had worked. He lit a cigarette as she assured him he did not want to be the last one to get involved.

At the end he said: 'But they are idiots. I don't care what any other publisher does.'

Emily started to scratch the skin at the edge of her thumbnail. She felt a droplet of sweat skitter down her vertebrae. Should she cut straight to a coercive 'time's running out' and say her goodbyes, or veer off into the personal approach, her last resort?

Before she could decide, Marcel Duliège twisted backwards, grunting, in his chair, to pull a tatty songbook from a long, teak side table clothed in music magazines, lever arch files, and an assortment of brown envelopes. On its cover was a photo, taken in the 1970s, of a pillow-lipped man wrapped in a chunky cardigan and hugging an acoustic guitar like it was a small child.

'You don't know who he is, do you?'

A-ha! thought Emily. Yes, I do. I've done my homework.

'He's one of the most famous sixties folk singers in France.' Dammit. She couldn't remember his name.

'Do you like folk music?'

This was easily fudged.

'It's not my favourite genre but I like certain artists.'

'What was the last record you played, Miss Quinn?'

Arse.

She ummed, looked out of the window, went blank. As she blinked slowly, it was as though the whole city had stopped, rocked back on its heels, and was gazing up at the window for her answer. She scrolled through her days, her weeks, the seven and a half months since she pulled into the

4

Gare du Nord, her brother's old InterRail rucksack at her feet. She could recall much panicked running down of Metro steps, much twirling miserably on her swivel chair at the office, queueing for sandwiches, getting home late, daydreaming of curly French autographs on dotted lines and then nightdreaming that she was locked all alone in a stuffy, windowless changing room. She could recall no playing of records. There hadn't been time. 'I don't know,' she said. The city looked away and resumed its course, again.

Suddenly, something cold was pressing against her knuckles. Marcel Duliège was forcing a glass of Ricard on her and smiling. She stared at it dumbly, as though she had just been handed someone else's wallet. He's not buying it, she thought. Or rather he's not buying me. I'm a phoney and he knows it. I can't do my job. I've never not been able to do something before. I will be fired. I too will do the march of the frog.

'You have –' he paused, nodding at her laptop, 'all that.' He lifted an arm – '*I* have all this' – and twirled an imaginary lasso. Emily looked around the room properly for the first time. Ceiling-to-floor bookcases filled two walls. Novels and fat biographies – Beethoven, Brel, the Beatles – crammed the top half. Tall, paperback songbooks whose spines had faded with age and sunshine ran all along the lower shelves like giant piano keyboards with only white keys. Propped up on the dusty, three-inch gap between the books and the edge of the shelves were postcards from Marrakesh, New York, Galway, Courcheval, London. There was one of the Mona Lisa, who looked pityingly at Emily, as if she was the only one not in on the wheeze. The remaining wall space was covered in framed posters of concerts at Olympia and the Elysée Montmartre, and photographs of Marcel Duliège with his songwriters: including, naturally, one of the most famous sixties folk singers in France. There they were on the Hippy Trail, young and chestnut and bare-chested. Chinking glasses at a black-tie awards ceremony with Simone Signoret. Receiving a gold disc. Fishing.

'I have managed for thirty years without digital downloading.' It wrongfooted her still further to hear the jargon spill so fluently from his mouth. 'And I am reluctant to move forward, as you put it, just for the sake of it.'

'But Mr Duliège,' hurried Emily, a new tack, a lifeline, coming to her at last. 'Your songwriters will expect you to – shouldn't you do what is best for them and their sales figures?'

'If you cannot ever find time to browse for a songbook,' he replied, leaning so far in she could smell the aniseed on his breath, 'you do not really love music. You do not really love life.'

She arched her eyebrows, unsure whether he was joking or not.

'And I . . .' he continued, before she could interject, 'do not cater for such people.'

Personal touch? What the hell. She had nothing more to lose now.

'Then I'm in big trouble.'

'I know.'

'Do you?'

'Of course I do. You have to sign me up. They've been after me for months. If you don't sign me up you don't stand a chance of signing anyone bigger than me and then, poof, no website. You're in trouble. I understand. Drink your Ricard.'

Emily did as she was told, her shoulders slumped, all pretence at businesslike prowess not only out the window, but down there on the muddy bed of the canal and tangled up in the laces of an old tramp's boot. So she told him she knew she was banging her head against a brick wall with his sort. Some of them didn't even really know what the internet was. In 1999! When she opened her computer, they frowned at her as if she'd opened a grubby trenchcoat to reveal rows of stolen wristwatches. That she needed one, just one, signature and the rest would follow – and if that first one was his then she, personally – forget about the Americans for a second – would do everything in her power to make sure he felt it had been worth it.

At the end he said: 'I just don't want to be part of the internet revolution.'

It was so hopeless it was almost funny. She leaned back on the cushions and tossed him a rueful smile, imagining herself clearing her desk of its scant personal effects and avoiding eye contact with a row of scornful colleagues sipping coffee and – quite possibly – booing and hissing. Moving out of her modern executive flat, of course, and in with, say, some Sorbonne students called Claudine and Gigi. Getting a job with a pinny in the restaurant on the corner of her road. Spending her first day's wages on some art supplies. Meeting a *beau garçon* and strolling in the Tuileries with him. She wanted to translate her life fully into French – real French, not this pidgin version she'd settled for.

'But I guess I must.'

What? She bolted upright again, so fast an icy slug of Ricard lurched from her glass and soaked through her skirt.

'I feel like the last foot soldier defending the walls of an ancient city whose inhabitants have all fled. Someone will wear me down eventually. It might as well be you. At least you will have a drink with me.'

7

Like watching a video on rewind, she saw herself drop the *beau garçon*'s hand, totter backwards out of the Tuileries at high speed, rip off her pinny and reverse into the office, scatter her pens and dictionaries back on the desk and flump down on her swivel chair. It was horrible.

'So, hand it over. Let me sign the damn thing.' He held out his palm and beckoned at her, as if trying to get a collar on a cat.

'Wait,' said Emily.

In the street below a small boy cried, 'Go, go!'

'You don't need this.' She took the contract from her bag and shook it once in front of his face. Then, looking him in the eye, she tore it up in long, slow movements. 'And nor do I.'

She paused, allowing the dramatic gesture to sink in, holding the paper streamers aloft and pondering whether to toss them giddily into the air or throw them petulantly out of the window. Seeing her dilemma, Marcel Duliège fetched the waste paper bin and nodded at her to drop them in, where they coiled themselves around a brown banana skin and some pencil shavings.

She took his arm as they walked down the stairs, and in the hallway they grasped each other's elbows and kissed on both cheeks. Spring was waiting beyond the door to bound alongside her in its warm, wet-nosed way to the place she had to go to do the thing she had to do. She reeked of Ricard, and had no job, but there were a thousand francs in her wallet. And she was positive the Mona Lisa had winked at her on the way out.

BRENDA EISENBERG

Under the Black Hat

Two young men slipped into the synagogue. Both in black hats, black coats, white shirts and beards. Late for the service, although just in time for the start of the Sabbath. Without looking round, they walked briskly to seats on either side of the synagogue. Despite their full beards, there was something child-like, perhaps almost guilty, about the way they entered, easing the door open, making a gap that was only just wide enough to slip through. Rachel had heard the stories, like everyone else, of what went on in some of the seminaries – now, as before, she tried not to think of it.

The first fellow was slim as a book: one of those thin hardbacks for women that addressed one topic only, such as the observances of the Sabbath, or the dietary laws, thought Rachel. His beard was neat and dark, his face pale, and he wore two decisive slashes for eyebrows, like a *mezuzah* and its mirror image. There'd been a *mezuzah* on the doorpost of her parents' home, a thin metal case fixed at a slant, but they were secular Jews and until recently she'd never thought of it, hardly even knew it was there. It was only when she sold the place and the Rabbi came to remove it that she understood from him that inside the case there was a little scroll of parchment with a prayer on it, that you should kiss the case whenever you walked past it, to remind you to remember God at all times, in all your dealings. Even though she tried hard to remember this, there were still occasions, Rachel reflected, when she walked past a *mezuzah* without seeing it.

The slim dark fellow had disappeared out of view somewhere on the benches behind the podium. The other one was ginger and slightly plump. His face hung more loosely from his hat, and he'd pushed at the door in a series of little judders, as if he couldn't quite be sure how much space he needed to squeeze himself through. Rachel watched as he manoeuvred past a line of congregants and chose a position below where she herself was sitting, in the women's gallery. He opened his prayerbook, turned to face the ark, closed his eyes, and began swaying from side to side. He had a wide mouth, with small, gappy teeth. Prayers were torrenting out of it now.

They were both *bochrim*, the term used for the devout young men, many of them rabbinical students, who were at the heart of this congregation. They were the ones who spent hours discussing the sacred texts, who prayed three times a day, who never let a piece of food or a sip of drink past their lips without a preceding prayer. They were the ones who worked hard at encouraging their more secular fellow-congregants to come twice a week to synagogue instead of once, even better, come three times. The ones who visited every home in the community before the major festivals, with a little gift and a laminated card summarising the appropriate observances. The ones who circulated lists of kosher foods, and ran study sessions for the wives about the dietary laws. Most of them were very young, Rachel had noticed. All dark hats and solemn expressions, teetering on teenage frames. Once she'd caught a glimpse of one of them, spinning down a corridor on his skateboard, his ritual fringes flying.

Rachel slipped off a shoe. She was wearing new shoes and the ten-minute walk to the synagogue from where she lodged, in a house the congregation kept for older single women, had left the backs of her heels raw. Using a car on the Sabbath was a particular issue in this congregation. Not only was it a blatant transgression of the laws of the Sabbath, but a clutter of cars in the car park, a roar of engines coming and going, was unconducive, said the Rabbi in sermon after sermon, to a peaceful atmosphere on the Sabbath. He talked about the health benefits of walking, he teased the lazy, he ranted at those who disagreed, he enlisted the support of the *bochrim* and gradually his campaign had made an impact. Now, less than six months since the start of his campaign, there were only a few diehards, not even a tenth of the congregation, that persisted with their cars.

While the ginger fellow continued praying alone, the rest of the congregation joined together in song. She heard one old man's voice rise above the swell of voices, drawing out the words, slowing down the song. It was, in any event, a restful song, sung together as a congregation week after week, and soothing, like a soak in a hot bath. The song came to an end, and the gappy young man also finished his prayer. He bowed either side of him, stepped forward, and the torrent, abruptly, was over.

He sat down, one arm slung across the back of his neighbour's chair, the other on his armrest, tapping in time to the singing. Behind him sat a boy of about six, alone for a few minutes while his father went to the men's room, and growing bored, which meant that he now reached up and smacked the brim of the big black hat in front of him. The hat tipped forwards, covering the *bocher*'s eyes. A mat of flat ginger hair showed on the back of his head. The boy jiggled up and down, his face fit to burst from grinning. His victim didn't move. The six-year-old turned up to the ladies' gallery, looking for an audience to share his delight. Then he swivelled back in his seat. The ginger head remained still as stone. The boy's glee began to wane. He held his fist to his mouth. Gnawed at it. Looked from left to right, wondering whether to make a run for it. Just then the *bocher* lifted his hat up, right off his head, whirled around and plonked it full square on the boy's head. And held it there for a few seconds, his hand flat on the crown of the hat. Forehead and eyes and nose and giggles trapped under the weight of the big black hat. Then he whipped it off, winked at the boy and settled it back on his own head again.

Rachel hadn't quite got the hang of this yet. One moment everything intense, the next, nothing but jovial. From darkness to light. In a flash. Right now was for joking, but next thing he'd be up on his feet, face up to the chandeliers, body swinging from side to side as if the force of one prayer was the only thing left on this earth that could keep the whole desperate business from imploding.

When everyone stood up for the next prayer, Rachel found herself looking out for the slim dark fellow, and there he was, standing on the opposite side of the synagogue. He had turned sideways to face his neighbour, an elderly man saying the *kaddish* for his wife. Rachel recognised his voice as the old man who was slowing things down before. Now he said the memorial prayer in chorus with a small group of other bereaved men, and again he was slow. Much slower than the rest, so that by the time they had finished, he still had a couple of passages to go, and was praying entirely on his own. It was near the end of the service, when the etiquette was to hurry things along, but the old man slowed down even more, as if the prayer itself was time, and he was determined to eke it out, note after juddering note. The dark young man still stood sideways, his eyes locked on to the old man, nodding and swaying in time to his chanting, his face betraying nothing but focus.

'Amen!' chorused the congregation as the old man came to an end. Loudly. Heartily. 'Amen!' It was almost spectacular, this heartiness. Packed full of the empathy of a congregation who'd known his wife and seen his loss (after all, didn't everyone know about loss?) and also, equally, bursting with the knowledge of what was laid out on the tables in the next-door hall: the chopped herring and fried fish balls and plaited breads and crisps and Coke and Fanta and boiled sweets and bottles of whisky. Lying deliciously on the other side of this act of remembrance, hardly six or seven minutes away.

As a woman, she herself had not been able to say *kaddish* for her own parents, who'd died one after the other, the summer before last. They were a small family, with no relatives. No male ones, anyway, so there was no one to say the *kaddish* prayer. Not until one of the *bochrim* volunteered to say it, as was required, three times a day every day for a year. The Rabbi had introduced them at the cemetery gates.

'This is Reuben,' the Rabbi had said.

The young man rubbed his thumb against one of the few tufts of dark hair on his chin, nodding his head as if he were already in prayer.

'Pleased to meet you,' Rachel said, clasping her hands

together so they wouldn't reach to shake his. He looked barely twenty.

On Friday nights and Saturday mornings she stood in the synagogue and watched and listened as he said the *kaddish* prayer. Remembering her parents, more assiduously, perhaps, than she herself did. And then, when the service was over, he always made a point of coming up to her, to wish her a Good Sabbath. One week it was announced that Reuben was engaged to be married. After the service that day, he introduced Rachel to his wife-to-be, a pale girl in large glasses, whose age she guessed to be seventeen or eighteen. I didn't know you had a girlfriend, Rachel nearly said. Now, every week they approached her together. Don't worry about saying it any more, Rachel wanted to say to him, now that you're getting married. It had almost been a relief when the year came to an end, and Reuben said his last *kaddish*. He still greeted her, although she noticed that occasionally he didn't.

The congregation took their seats for announcements. Rachel sat down with relief, and slipped off her shoes again. It had seemed natural, after her parents died, to step into the embrace of the congregation. Taking on the religious observances was a small price to pay, wasn't it? And anyway, it had happened gradually. First, they'd suggested she attend a couple of evening classes for women. That was where she'd been given her little library of slim hardbacks, each on a different topic: The Sabbath; The Dietary Laws; Cleanliness for Women; The High Holy Days. At the classes they'd stressed the importance of synagogue attendance, and so Rachel started coming to the Sabbath services. And of course, there was the injunction not to work on the Sabbath. 'No Jew,' her teacher (a woman with grey hair moulded into scrolls above her temples) explained, 'may work on the Sabbath, not even to make a fire. So we never light a spark on the Sabbath. Not unless it's a spiritual spark,' and her grey lips stretched into a smile. 'In other words, we don't switch on a light, we don't watch the television, and we don't use a car.'

The old widower, the slow singer, was one of the few who'd not changed his ways when it came to driving on the Sabbath. 'It's because of his Jaguar,' people said. 'From where he lives the walk must take barely ten minutes. It's not even as if he's in bad health,' they said. Sure enough, Rachel had seen him drawing into the car park this evening, a small man set back far inside a cocoon of humming gold. On its bonnet, the exuberant jaguar, caught in mid-pounce.

The announcements were still in full flow. Two barmitzvahs this week, and a dinner for the whole congregation, co-sponsored by the two proud pairs of parents. *Mazeltov!* And an engagement. And a new grandchild. And no fewer than five students had excelled in their end of school exams. *Mazeltov! Mazeltov! Mazeltov!* The congratulations crash-landed into the room, loud and slapdash. Each joyous event another little hurdle before a sip of sweet wine and a forkful of cheesecake.

The announcements were over, there was another round of *kaddish* and the congregants closed their prayerbooks, kissed the covers, leaned back in their seats and erupted into the last song of the service. *Yigdal Elokim Chai.* Praise the living God, they sang.

At the dinner, Rachel noticed that the two young men who'd slipped in together now sat together, side by side, close to the Rabbi. Eyes closed, singing hard, rocking in unison. What was in their heads, Rachel wondered, as she watched them. In all of their devout young heads, pressed like flowers, between beards and hats? There were times when they looked deep in reverie, when she was sure they'd flown to heaven. But other times, their mouths slid fast and aggressive round the sacred verses, like rally cars cornering tightly – a race to get to the end of the prayer. Yes, she'd heard the stories, like everyone else, of what went on in some of these seminaries – she tried now, harder than ever, not to think of it.

The Rabbi and the *bochrim* started singing Sabbath songs, and one by one the congregants drifted out, to make their way home. Rachel sat down on a low wall outside the synagogue, and took off a shoe. The leather around the heel was hard as a shell. It had grazed away the skin on the back of her heel. She rubbed the pink wound through her stockings. Then took off the other shoe and worked each heel in turn between thumb and forefinger, trying to pinch some of the stiffness out of the leather. Opposite, there was a cluster of men in the evening gloom. These days most people gave the car park a wide berth – it had the feel of something excommunicated about it, during the Sabbath. But tonight there was quite a gathering there, with the old man and his Jaguar and a growing buzz at the centre of it. From inside the hall the chorus of a song drifted out. The buzz from the car park got louder. Rachel slipped her shoes back on.

There was a gate at the far end of the car park and Rachel decided to head for it, taking her directly past the group of men. She stood up, slinging her weight forward on to the balls of her feet to relieve her heels. As she got close, she peered through their heads. The old man was kneeling now, in a position that looked like some form of gentile worship, with one hand laid across the tyre of his car. What Rachel saw next, under the grey light of the lamppost, made her feel like the rawness on her heels had

16

ignited, the sore now creeping up her legs, her trunk, her arms, her head. There on the tyre, below the old man's quivering hand, was a slash, a long and thin and slanting slash – in a shape that was not at all different from an eyebrow, or a *mezuzah*.

KATIE BARRON

The Chickens and the Lettuces

GREG HAD had chickens for a while. They were splodges of orange in their pen at the bottom of his garden. The London clay had been scratched bare by those gnarled and greedy feet so that you could see bits of brick and mortar and green glass showing through. After a while, when they had finished a spot of scratching, they just stood, their plumage fluffed up around them under the spitting rain, their beaks turned towards the house and Greg, where he lay soaking in an antique bath in the middle of the kitchen. He let them wait.

They were a bit of a nuisance to tell the truth. The fox had got one and Greg had been obliged to improve and deepen the fencing. And they required regular feeding. But he got cred with his friends. It was an eccentric activity, which seemed to match the house: nearly two hundred years old and a third of that time inhabited by one man, Greg's predecessor. The man had left behind him sixteen clocks when he was finally hauled off to his repose in a nursing home. The man hadn't been young when he moved into the house but he was old when he left. Greg had a sort of feeling for the guy, and attempted to keep all sixteen clocks ticking. Saturday morning, after a hard night's drinking, was clock-winding time, except for the cuckoo clock which he left till later in the day when he felt stronger. And on Saturday afternoons he could be seen sometimes on the Farringdon Road looking for the old clock mender until he packed up shop; or on Sunday mornings in Brick Lane rootling through the wooden drawers of bits in search of a cog or a pendulum. Not that he cared that much for clocks himself and he did live with a quiet fear that the old man's spirit was knocking on the doors of his body for entry, might seep in through the vapours of his hot baths. But it was something to do.

The chickens with their beaks turned towards the house felt the time could be better spent feeding them. What was a wooden cuckoo beside a live bantam hen?

For Sarah it was all kinky, spoke to her of openings and cracks and discoveries. Fifteen years younger than Greg, she slipped in easily, first time he opened the front door. Mugs of tea and dawdling, trying out the jukebox, visiting the chickens, ogling the clocks. She hung around until it finally dawned on him there was an opportunity here. He dug her long hair and jeans. He couldn't believe his luck.

Sarah moved in soon after, full of fantasies of a life of bliss amid love and clocks and chickens. She had never had a home of her own. Now she started to gaze happily at the empty flowerbeds and she conceived the plan of planting a vegetable garden. She would start with lettuces, then later other things. She had never had a patch of earth into which she could plant something and watch it grow. 'Go ahead,' said Greg. So Sarah bought the seeds one day when they were in Southwold and she took advice. She drew a long trench in the clay, parallel with the wall of old black bricks, added some compost, sprinkled the seeds and covered it over.

The chickens knew she was up to something. On the days when Greg left the gate of their enclosure ajar, they wandered out, apparently casually, but soon all took up position on the site of Sarah's lettuces. They scratched and pecked but the seeds were too deep down. They tilted their heads and eyed each other in case one of the others had hit on a solution that she was trying to keep to herself.

Sarah felt uneasy. She didn't feel her lettuces were going to have much of a chance. That pack of bantams was intimidating if nothing else. 'Please remember to shut the gate, Greg,' she said.

'Sure,' said Greg, reading the paper. But next day the catch still wasn't properly done up and the gate swung open again.

'How come you always remember at night,' asked Sarah, 'when it's a question of keeping the foxes out, but in the morning, when it's about protecting my lettuces, you don't bother?'

This was the clarion call. Greg recognised it of old and sighed deep within his being. Women were never happy, they were never still, they never let you read the paper. He pushed back his plate where the red sauce that Heinz puts on its baked beans was congealing under the knife. They had feasted on home-produced eggs (he was proud of them) in a breakfast that was decadently late considering that it was a working day. He eyed Sarah from behind the half-empty plastic milk bottle and weighed up possible approaches. Knowing her as he did, he decided the best tack was to adopt a high moral tone. 'Don't you think the chickens deserve a bit of space to run around in? How would you like to be a bantam cooped up in a pen all day with nothing to do but wait for the next meal? It's nice for them to get out and feel the grass under their feet, strut their stuff.'

'OK, but if you thought that, why did you say to me to go ahead and plant lettuces? I've put all the effort in and now the chickens are going to muck it up.'

Morality hadn't worked. Greg tried male superiority. He broadened his pecs and pointed one shoulder towards her in a half shrug. 'Those chickens won't harm your lettuces, I promise you. You really don't have to worry.'

'So you're not going to close the gate?'

Time for patience. He nodded gently in relationship counsellor mode. 'I think chickens and plants can co-exist.' Then, to show he was taking her seriously, he put in some evidence: 'Chickens have been around for centuries.'

'In coops.'

She had an answer for everything this girl. He shifted up a gear, from relationship counsellor to psychotherapist. 'I don't think this is about chickens. I think there's something in you you want to keep cooped up. Something you want to keep under control. Otherwise you couldn't possibly get upset like this.'

'I want my lettuces to grow,' said Sarah.

'Fine. So do I.'

He saw that she was relenting slightly. He wondered which of his arguments had had its effect.

'We could make a bigger coop,' she said.

Ah. So her tender heart was feeling for the chickens. 'I am not going to build a bigger chicken coop. It took me six weeks to build that one and that's the only coop I'm going to build.' He felt the weight of the world's coop-building on his shoulders. A cross he and a select few had to bear together. He shook his newspaper to underline the dignity of the guild of coop-builders and to signal the end of the interview.

Sarah left the room. He could hear her upstairs taking a vigorous shower. For some reason she disdained to use the antique bathtub that kept them company here in the kitchen at all their candlelit dinners. The candles were romantic but also necessary at times when the electricity in the house refused to function.

Sarah appeared again at the door. Her wet hair fell down on either side of her face and her green eyes looked at him anxiously. Her hands fidgeted with each other. 'The lettuces are important to me,' she said, looking down at her bracelets and then across to him again.

He crossed the room and loved her up a bit, soothed her arms. 'Of course, gorgeous girl,' he said. 'I know.' She smiled and they smooched some more.

Left alone after Sarah had gone to work, Greg felt cross. He didn't know why women always had to set up these tests: 'If you don't do this, you don't love me.' He knew he had to put his foot down hard now, because if not it would start with lettuces and it would end God knows where. At first she was happy with his set-up. Now she was starting the proverbial female activity of changing things. He sighed and let himself into his bath, his mug of tea poised dangerously on the edge. It was only bare floorboards underneath so it didn't really matter. The chickens waited.

When he went out to feed the chickens that morning he shut the gate properly after him. He hated himself for doing it. He knew it wasn't because he agreed with her but just because of an uneasy fear that if he put a foot wrong he might lose her. Women were unpredictable. Anything could make them fly off the handle. He gazed at the chickens through the chicken wire. They were marching up and down behind it like sentries on a border. He wondered how soon he and Sarah would start to need passports to cross over into each other's territories.

Over the coming days Greg bounced back and forth across the line of danger. Most of the time he shut that gate. Occasionally he forgot. Sarah wrung his neck

23

jokingly. She weeded her patch once a week. One day she was wandering about the slimy lawn barefoot when she noticed the verdant spots on the earth. She jumped up and down in excitement. 'They've sprouted!' she called up to the man in the bath.

Every day they swelled. The slugs took great bites out of them. Sarah hauled the slugs off and dribbled gravel around the lettuce patch so they wouldn't come back. 'Why don't you use slug pellets?' Greg asked, but it was only to wind her up because he knew it would be against her principles.

'I'm worried about your chickens,' she said lightly.

'Chickens aren't stupid,' said Greg, 'and anyway, don't you trust me?'

They were getting on well, so well in fact that Sarah wanted to have her parents round to lunch. 'Good idea,' said Greg but he felt a little uneasy in the stomach for no reason he could put a finger on. Then he realised why. Sarah was eyeing the bathtub. She said it was arty and eccentric 'n' all but it hampered their social life. There wasn't space for a proper table. Candlelit dinners for two were all they could stretch to. Where would her parents eat their lunch?

Greg was cornered. There was no other socially acceptable solution than to move his bath. If they were going steady, parents would have at some stage to be invited. Even he didn't really want to look like a weirdo to Middle England. As he prepared to disengage the pipes, Sarah looked at him sorrowfully. 'Maybe we could fix it up in one of the bedrooms,' she suggested. Maybe, but that would involve getting a plumber and spending a bomb. He wasn't that desperate. He wasn't a fetishist. No, bourgeois respectability was just the price you paid for sex. Not that it was only about sex, this thing with Sarah.

'I know!' he said. 'We can put it in the coop. We can give

the old queens a dust bath. They'll love it.' He grinned. And so they did. Sarah and Greg filled it with sawdust and it was just low enough for the creatures' clipped wings to take them to the rim. Then they let themselves down inside and got shimmying until the dust had penetrated every follicle. Sarah and Greg went back to the new improved kitchen and examined recipe books and selected roast chicken with cranberries for the important Sunday lunch. Then they got down to some shimmying themselves.

The day after he had donated the bath to the chickens, Greg forgot to check the catch on the door of their enclosure. He was in good spirits after the previous evening, was whistling a tune and wasn't as late for work as usual. All seemed fine with the world.

Once lord and master was out of the house, those hens strutted out with the confidence of five Miss Americas. Nothing could please them more than the sight of the tender shoots in the lettuce patch. Gravel was nothing to them. It barely moved under their greedy feet. All day they scratched and pecked. They even took an out-of-bounds dust bath, as the earth was dry. It was even more fun than the legally sanctioned one. Then off they trotted back to the coop.

When Sarah got back that evening she found her young lettuces gone, and the gate of wood and chicken wire swinging on its hinges. The chickens acted as if nothing had happened. So did Greg. 'There wasn't much leafage there anyway. It hadn't started growing for real yet . . .'

'My effort was for nothing,' said Sarah through tears of fury as she flung her few clothes into a couple of holdalls.

'Where are you going?'

'You could have told me straight that you weren't going to keep the gate closed. We could have built a fence just for the lettuces.'

'Why are you going?'

'Do I ask much here really, Greg? Do I ask for electricity, do I ask for central heating, do I ask for dinner at the Ritz?'

'Why are you leaving?'

'I just wanted to grow some lettuces.' Tears flowed down her beautiful cheeks. Surely he must wake up from this surreal nightmare! But she went.

'I wanted to grow lettuces,' was her parting shot, as she stood for the last time in the doorway.

That was it. That was it with women. Greg stormed out to the chicken coop, rinsed out the bath with the hose. 'Sorry, ladies,' he said. 'We're back to plan A.' He reinstated the bath, and himself in it.

The chickens tiptoed out and around. They played grand-ma's footsteps, fearing to be shooed back. But no one shooed them back. They went so regularly to the lettuce patch that the gravel eventually mixed in with the earth to make a homogeneous surface. They attacked with fury every time a lettuce plant tried again to reach the light.

Greg soaked in his bath. Fourteen or fifteen clocks ticked on, dividing the time that stretched ahead into equal portions. They sent their nervous voices out on zigzag pathways through the house, rising to a crescendo on the hour and falling away again to a repetitive patter. Greg tried to read. He wondered idly to himself what lettuces might taste like fresh from the garden. He would have liked to know.

EMILY PERKINS

How Do You Tell
When a Person's Broken?

JONAS WAS seven years old and therefore at the develop-
mental stage for persistent joke-telling. His father John,
at forty-five, was developing in the opposite direction,
which made him frequently lose items that were in his
hands or on his head; he was unable to find this in
the least funny. Jonas's younger sister Elizabeth was
in the phase of learning to lie, and their mother, John's
wife Penelope, was going through a period – not her first,
but the most prolonged to date – of considering adultery.
The chronic cause of her drifting, so far theoretical,
unfaithfulness was her husband's perpetual unemployment
'outside the home', but needling it acutely was the looming
prospect of time alone together. A week from now, the
Henleys were going on holiday.

There were lists all over the kitchen that said things like 'J
recorder', 'leg wax Friday' and 'new sheets for Melanie'.
This was John's sister, who was coming to stay in the house
while they were away. It was a win-win situation, as she and
her depressed husband, David, got to have a break in
London, and John was able to indulge a familial fellow-
feeling without actually having to endure his sister's company. Melanie drank, and when she was around, Penelope
drank too, and then both of them hectored John about what

he was doing with his life. 'I'm raising our children,' he would say, 'what do you think I'm doing?'

'Yes, but we could pay someone to do that,' Penny would reply.

'Oh fuck off. I don't want to.'

'Hmm.'

In the morning she would apologise. 'I'm sorry. You're amazing with the kids. I'm sorry for being such an arse.'

'Nice arse.' He'd make the obligatory swipe for it with the tea towel and she would duck away rather more quickly than she should. Melanie would emerge, her eyes puffed. Penelope hated to think what sort of dreams she had.

Once, when Jonas was a tiny baby, David had taken an overdose in the middle of the night when staying in their spare room. It had been a long time before he was allowed to stay again, and he was only welcome on assurances that he was taking all his medication. These days John and Penny wondered whether they had been too harsh, too much in the throes of uptight new parenthood to be properly understanding of David's pain. Oh well, it had happened that way, and 'I'm not a perfect person,' Penny often said, as though she was doing a night school course in self-forgiveness. The after effect was that David, somewhat guiltily, adored Jonas and would listen to his jokes for hours. Over the years, as Melanie's love for David was unswerving, even if she did drink, John and Penny had come to love him too, and now felt sure that their home was a place in which he would never harm himself.

The Henleys left London every summer for their little cottage in the last unfashionable Suffolk village, which Penelope's grandfather had bequeathed to her in the absence of love for his own children. This had been awkward for the first few years; she had invited her mother and father to join them there at Christmases but no, the hurt was too great, and for some time she and John thought it best to sell the house and buy another property nearby. But after several holidays there – cracking nuts in front of the minuscule fire, or taking Thermoses of tea on the long grey sands – the cottage seemed filled with them, with their John-and-Penelope-ness, and the idea of selling it too great a sacrifice. 'I'm not a perfect person,' said Penelope to her mother and father. 'You know you are welcome to Suffolk at any time.' ('As if she owned the county,' said Penny's mother.) In the days before Jonas and Elizabeth the puddingy old double bed upstairs was somewhere they particularly liked to make love; now it was the only place on God's green earth in which they made love. This was one reason why John was looking forward to the holiday.

'Dad, where do vampires go to college?'

'I don't know. Where do they go to college?'

'Fright school!'

'Have you done your homework?'

'Don't have any. Last week of term.'

'Don't you have exams or something?'

'Dad. I'm seven.'

'Fuck. We're going to be late to the station.'

'You swore.'

'Thanks, Libby, I know. Have you seen my car keys?'

'No.'

Penelope heaved three straining Waitrose bags on to the kitchen bench.

'Melanie wants to know which restaurants we like at the moment,' John said. 'I told her the last time we went out for dinner was in 1998.'

29

'There's a very good new Argentinian place down Rose-bery Ave.' Penelope paused to kiss her sister- and brother-in-law hello. 'Near the registry office. John, could you give me a hand please, there's loads more in the taxi.'

It was a steaming evening. John dreaded the next day's journey. They would rise at five, pack, flick the switch on the children who would instantly waken with full-daylight energy, plug them into the back seat and muffle them with their own headphones. That afternoon they had been an hour late to collect David and Melanie from the train. John had very nearly been in tears before Elizabeth showed him where she'd hidden the car keys.

The taxi driver sat smoking into the thick grey heat, the back door of his cab open to reveal a mountain of grocery bags.

'Christ. Will all of this fit in the chiller?'

'Melanie and David can eat what we can't take.'

'You didn't have to do that.'

Penelope shrugged. Melanie and David struggled to make ends meet, and leaving them with a full larder assuaged the peculiar guilt they made her feel.

'Melanie said on the way back from the station that there's a shop interested in stocking her clothes.'

'They will live in Hastings,' Penelope said, 'where nobody wants beautiful things. Melanie should be in London.'

'They like the sea.'

'They can holiday by the sea, like normal people do.'

When she was like this, John thought of his wife, the thing to sort her out would be a good fuck. She was insecure, that was Pen's problem, she worked fantastically hard, her interiors shop was a success, and she was highly strung and every now and then needed to be treated like a woman. Melanie, who was comfortable in her own booze-

30

soaked skin, made her nervous, and Penny put on a show when she was around. It was John's job, he knew, to make things all right. He'd been so tired lately . . . But no more excuses. Poor, patient Penelope. This holiday he would spoil her. Breakfast in bed. Get the teenager from the chip shop to baby-sit and take her to that Michelin-starred place that had featured in the paper.

Back in the house, Penelope pulled him into the hallway, a low thrill in her voice like a schoolgirl at a party. 'I've just had a brilliant idea.' She whispered in his ear.

'What did you say?'

She repeated herself; the husky aspirants and her water-melon perfume made him blink. He lifted his gaze to her eyes, opalescent blue like one of those Swedish glass gew-gaws she sold for heart-stopping prices.

'Are you mad? No. This is our holiday. Everything's planned.'

Penelope dropped her voice low. 'John. Let's be generous. Just this one year. You know we ought to share the cottage more.'

Ought they? Was this all about her parents? 'Maybe they won't want to.'

'Let's ask them.'

Just as helplessly as he had been steered out of the kitchen, John was now steered back into it to face his sister, who was washing the children's supper dishes, and David, eyes fixed on the *Guardian* Sudoku.

'Oh Melanie, John will do those.' Penelope unscrewed the top of a pale green bottle. 'God, I'm dying for a glass of wine.' She poured three large glasses. David couldn't drink wine and take his medication. Occasionally he swapped one for the other, but disaster usually followed.

'So here's my suggestion.' Everyone was watching

Penelope. She hadn't eaten since lunch, and the first mouthful of wine gave her a pleasant little buzz. She enunciated slowly, the announcer of the grand prize on a reality TV contest. 'How about you both come to the cottage for a holiday with us?' There was a pause, during which she decided not to gauge the room but to keep on going. 'Don't stay in smelly hot old London with all the tourists, come and have a break by the seaside.'

'We live by the seaside,' Melanie laughed.

'Yes, but this would be a holiday. Please. We'd love to – you know, cook for you, and show you our favourite spots.' Emotion swelled Penelope's heart. 'We never see enough of you, and you've . . .' she was going to say 'done so much for us', but then couldn't think of an example and in the interests of honesty said, 'always been important in our lives.'

'Thank you, Pen,' said Melanie in her dry way, 'that's very touching. But don't you want the holiday to yourselves?'

'We should think about transport,' said John, 'we can't all fit in our car.'

For a second Penelope was stumped. Then, 'Oh that's easy, you three drive and I'll take the train with the kids.'

Immediate protest. 'No, that's far too big a sacrifice . . .' 'You can't possibly . . .' 'The kids will be a nightmare on the train . . .' 'There won't be any decent seats left . . .'

'It'll be fine,' she said, pulling crackers out of a click-clack box and shaking them on to a plate as she continued, 'The kids can bunk down with us – and I'd like to take them on the train, it'll be an adventure.' Another pause. 'It's up to you of course. We don't have to decide right now.' Although school holidays . . . they would have to buy rail tickets as soon as possible. Suddenly she was embarrassed, as though she had gushed, and everyone thought her a fool. 'Anyway,' she said, 'I'm going to go and pack. John, have you done the children?' Oh *God*, it was like being on stage, she had to get away from these hateful people now and with any luck they would see her idiotic idea for what it was and politely turn her down.

'I'd like to go,' said David.

'Really?'

Melanie swigged her wine. 'Are you sure?'

'It'd be great. Fresh air, hanging out with the children. And you guys.'

'Fantastic!' Great! It would be just great. Penelope took the phone into her bedroom and rang her travel agent, who assured her that tickets could be biked round that very night, and at a fee so laughably high that she clutched the figure to her, polishing it to drop casually in to bedtime conversation with her husband. For it was surely – if further proof were needed – final confirmation of her generosity.

Every car roof in the supermarket car park sported a quizzical seagull, the birds seemingly posing for a seaside kitsch postcard. This was the part of English holidays that Penelope hated. At least at Leclerc or one of the Spanish hypermarkets you could pick up some dirt-cheap espadrilles and an amusing animal-shaped lilo for the pool. The East Anglian Tesco, on the other hand, was a horror. Even at this point in the summer, just a week into their holiday, the shelves were patchily stocked, there were no organic chickens left, and the sight of livid sunburnt backs and men with bellies like expectant women were a painful reminder that she was a terrible, helpless snob. Oh well! The shopping had to be done, and at least it was David who'd volunteered to come with her. She and John had agreed the night before that under no circumstances must they leave the children in Melanie's care. It turned out that for Melanie a holiday meant taking a break from any sobriety at all. It had been a bottle of wine with lunch; now it was a bottle of wine before lunch, then another one with lunch, which she barely ate. After that she tended to fall asleep in the sun – she had gone a lovely brown – before rousing herself around five to stand in the poky cottage kitchen drinking wine while Penny or John prepared the children's tea. The children ignored her completely, but spent hours combing the beach for treasures to bring David, delighted that he especially liked scuffed plastic bread bags and the silvery remnants of crisp packets.

'Look out,' David said as they pushed the laden trolley back towards the car. 'You nearly stepped in that sick.'

Penelope shuddered. 'Don't say sick.'

'Still too soon?'

The train trip had indeed been a disaster. Penelope and the children, down to their last change of clothes, had wound up getting off at Ipswich and taking a taxi the rest of the way. The cost was not worth thinking about. The folly of inviting David and Melanie was not worth thinking about. What was, was, and now they had to make the best of it.

'There's a junk shop near here I'd really like to have a quick fossick in, do you mind?'

'Do you think the food will be all right?'

'We'll park in the shade. I won't be long.'

Instantly she could see that the shop had nothing decent except perhaps some of the linen and a silver cutlery set that – look at the price! – she couldn't sell for very much more back in London. In between lifting bedsheets to gauge them for weight and check for stains, she glanced over at the dark smudgy tan on David's neck as he slowly traversed the

34

shelves of Victorian children's books. She looked away as he came towards her, a faded red hardback in his hands.

'Anything here?'

'No,' she said. He reached into the linen pile as though it were a lucky dip and pulled out a long piece of exquisite lace, not the best she had ever seen but probably the prettiest. My God, she thought, it's a wedding veil from Honiton, early nineteenth century at the latest.

'What about this?'

'Fuck,' she said softly, 'my God, you are a genius.'

'Is it worth a lot of money?'

'No, not very much,' she said firmly, aware the puggish shop owner was listening. 'What's that you've got?'

'Adventure stories for Jonas.'

'Right, and I might get –' she cast her eyes around '– this necklace.' Red glass beads, 1950s, badly strung but a beautiful fresh paint colour. Penelope tucked the veil under her arm carelessly, as if it were a beach towel. 'Let's see what she wants for the lot.'

Outside the sunshine was temporarily blinding. Penelope grabbed David by the wrist and pulled him round the corner, his legs stumbling after his body. In the shadow of a side street she jumped up and down on the spot, six years old suddenly, clapping her hands, short little squeals coming from her throat.

'What? Is it the veil?'

'Yes, yes, it's the fucking veil!' Penelope put her hands to her throat, then her cheeks, her eyes shining over the little mooned fingernails. She breathed in deeply. 'You are brilliant.'

'Oh my God oh my God, I'm so sorry we're late.'

'Mummy, we're *starving*.'

'There's no milk. I want milk.'

35

'Have you been drinking?' John took a Tesco bag from his wife.

'David has found the most wonderful thing. I bought it for the shop. Melanie! Is she awake?'

'Milk, Daddy, milk!'

'Just wait, Elizabeth, I'm opening it.'

'Melanie!'

'I'm here.'

John held the milk carton at arm's length and glugged it down the sink. 'This milk is off.'

Melanie leaned into the kitchen, her knuckles white around the door frame. 'Where have you two been?'

Penelope held out a folded square of tissue. 'For you.'

At four in the morning, her body hot and fizzing with sugar from too much wine, Penelope lay trying to forget the things she had said in the dark pub with David, giddy over that bad champagne. Those fatuous remarks about not being able to remember her wedding vows, even though it was true that the words of the civil ceremony had escaped her, and she genuinely wondered whether or not she had promised to be faithful, really what an idiotic and provocative thing to say. She didn't even fancy *Dave*, as he was to his own family – Mel and Dave, like a couple of cheesy old pub troubadours, and she and John the only people who persisted in using their full names. What else had she said – oh, terrible disloyal things. True but disloyal, like telling David how she felt when certain women came into the shop – women who didn't work, whose husbands were out earning money, whose children were with nannies – wringy with envy, fat and invisible at the same time, 'Like,' she had said, 'that stubby little shop lady in the junk shop back there.'

'I don't remember her.'

'Exactly!' And she had cackled. She was a terrible person.

Jonas, asleep on the stretcher bed, kicked and groaned. 'No, Libby, it's mine! No, Libby!'

In the morning John brought tea and toast. 'Oh darling, thank you.'

'How's your head?'

'I'm so sorry.'

'Tea's black, I'm afraid.'

The car had stunk of rotting fish when she and David had got back to it. Neither of them had felt okay to drive, but the sudden awareness of the time had stung her with the adrenaline necessary to get home. 'Do you think Melanie likes her necklace?'

'Yes, why not?'

'She didn't seem very pleased.'

'You'd just got her medicated husband drunk.'

'Is he all right?'

'Don't know.'

She looked at him through the grille of her fingers. 'I can't believe you said that about the money.'

'What, offering them a cut when you sell the veil? Why not?'

'It's embarrassing.'

'Why?'

'They're broke. It's like pity money.'

John snorted. 'No it's not! If – I don't know, if it were anyone else, Charlie and Lisa say, you'd offer them a finder's fee.'

'But it's not them. It's your sister, and they've got no money and it makes it insulting.'

'So because they're poor we've got to withhold cash from them? You're crazy.'

'David doesn't expect any money. Anyway it's theoretical until I sell it. Hello Jo.'

How long had he been standing there?

Jonas rubbed his eyes. 'What are you two talking about?'

'Nothing.'

'Why did the chicken cross the road?'

'I don't know.'

'To go to the shops.'

Elizabeth thundered in and leapt on her mother, showering dirt and bits of grass all over the bed.

'My tea, careful!'

'You promised we could go to the penny arcade.'

'Oh God, did I?'

'You promised, you promised!'

John grinned. 'Poor you.'

'Look, I'll tell you what children, let Mummy have a shower and we'll have a lovely morning in the kitchen baking.'

'You promised!'

And so it went on. In order to stop feeling like a terrible person Penelope took her children to the scuffed, dark penny arcade that smelled burningly of cheap sugar and cigarettes. Elizabeth's hand was moist and chubby in hers as they crossed the road towards the beach afterwards, to try and clear the headaches the children were now complaining of. Jonas ran ahead and down towards the thick grey waves, his arms stretched behind him, gunning for the gulls. Look at his long legs, the thin angles of his shoulders! He was a marvellous thing, swooping out there in the distance.

It wasn't until the children's bedtime that John, Penny and Melanie realised David had been gone, alone, all day. The four of them were due to go out to dinner. In the pause while they all absorbed this development the only sound was the soft Suffolk burble of the teenage girl from the chip shop, reading to Elizabeth on the sofa. Jonas was still in the bath.

'We'll miss our booking,' Penelope said. 'Oh fuck fuck fuck.'

'I'm sure they'll hold the table.' John tried to keep the darkness out of his voice and failed. 'They've got our credit card details. Where's a pen for fuck's sake?'

'You're holding one. Did he not say anything?' Penny stared at Melanie, willing her to snap out of her daze.

Jonas appeared with a towel around his shoulders. 'Daddy, how do you know when a person's broken?'

'Not now, Jo, I haven't time for jokes.' John paced the room, the mobile phone shoved against his ear.

'It's not a joke, it's a question.'

'Shh!'

'Go outside, John,' Penelope said.

'There's no fucking signal outfuckingside.'

'Mummy, how do you know when a person's broken?'

John spoke through clenched teeth. 'Shut up, everybody, I can't hear!'

'Don't tell the children to shut up.'

He looked as though he might hit her, then suddenly all his energy was sucked into the telephone. 'Hello? Yes, hello, I've got a reservation . . .'

Penelope drew Jonas to her, ran a hand over his damp hair. 'Now darling. What was it?'

'How do you know when a person's broken?'

She laughed. *She* was not tense, *she* would not tell the children to shut up or care about a Michelin reservation, she was full of maternal love and ready to listen to all the bad jokes in the world, if only David would come home right bloody now. 'I don't know, darling, how *do* you tell when a person's broken?'

'It's not a joke. I'm asking you.'

'He's asking you a question,' said Melanie.

'Like you and Daddy were talking about. How David's broken. How do you tell?'

'Libby!' Penelope crossed the room and slammed shut the book in the teenager's hands. Everyone froze. 'Libby, have you seen Uncle David tonight?'

The five-year-old blinked slowly. 'No,' she said.

She felt dreadful. She had been feeling dreadful for longer than she cared to remember. She was not a perfect person. That was why she was going, now, to the chest in the spare room where she had carefully folded the veil into tissue paper and placed it in a drawer. Melanie and David's suitcase sat in front of the chest, clothes and books exploding from it like stuffing from an ancient couch. Small, bright red blobs were scattered over the pile – the beads from that necklace – the string must have snapped. Penelope pushed the heavy suitcase aside with her foot. Acid rose in her stomach as she pulled the drawer open. She did not expect to see the veil. But there it was, the paper soft and white around it. Slowly she lifted the veil, careful to hold only the edges, shaking the tissue from it. Fifteen hundred pounds was probably its value, but in Islington she might get more. 'Oh, David,' she said out loud, 'where are you?' She held the soft net up towards the window, its faintly caramel antique colour picking up the last of the light left in the evening. Fifteen hundred pounds. If she could bear to part with it.

The road out of the village was lined with bushes, brambles, gorse that smelled even in the cool evening of honey. Behind him the lights of the Spar glowed white, slightly illuminating his way through the dusk. He had been waiting all day for the cotton wool to come in from the edges of space around him and wrap everything, muffle sensation, leave him alone and numb. But it seemed he had been lucky this time. There were so many sounds, the distant scrape of the waves, crickets, the falling liquid popping of a night-bird. People laughing from the pub, the faint growl of lorries on the road ahead. It would be too far to walk to the motorway, and he had no plan of walking too far. There was something else, another sound, a crackle over everything, cellophane light as though it was nothing but the movement of air. Maybe it was just the movement of air. This was what he would do, he thought: he'd walk further down this road, until it met another one, and then he would turn and head back to the house.

EMMA HENDERSON

A l'Ombre

Inez, mallory, Yvonne, Anna. These were the girls I loved. These were the girls who died.

1969 and all of us eleven, but only Inez wore a bra. She showed us it at break, the very first day at our posh girls' grammar school. It was checked, turquoise and white, cotton, and surprisingly soft to the touch. Inez called it a trainer bra and said we could buy them at Peter Jones. She had a lilac and white one too, she said, and they also came in pink and white, and yellow and white. Beneath the bra, bosoms round and hard as Coxes. Everybody loved Inez, or hated her. You couldn't help it. She was that sort of girl, the sort who stood out. Brown curly hair, cropped short, that bubbled when she talked, and marmite eyes whose whites were blue. She lived with her father – Papa – and a sisterly stepma in Phillimore Walk, W8. Most of us bussed it in from the mummyish suburbs, or commuted with brothers and dads, from the blue-green extremes of the Piccadilly and District lines: Sudbury Hill, North Ealing, South Ealing, Broadway and Common. But Inez, dizzy Inez: even her name was exotic, erotic, or seemed so to me. Inez Deleuze; velvety vowels, Beethoven's fifth, those two sexy z's. Was she Spanish or French? I did find that out. Her mother, she said, was Irish, dead. She said she was a love child, a bastard or a fitz. Her language was colourful, her sophistication irresistible. She showed us how to roll our skirts at the waistband to shorten them, how to loosen our ties to be cool and how to flip the collars of our blazers, like boys. Later, she swore we would shed several pounds by sweating, if we followed her example and wore, all summer term, thick knitted tights with an Aran pattern, loose at the knees, bristly on my own, bare thigh, on the stairs, our legs colliding – accidentally on purpose – hot and hairy. It was a theory of hers; she was full of them, full of herself too, and, without the tights, so smooth and appley: her cheeks, her calves – their shape and shine; her juicy buttocks, squadging in the changing room; wet hair; thick, warm air; thick, green, combed knickers, cidery with sweat. One April the first, Inez stole all the board rubbers: knubbly blocks of pale, unvarnished wood, with grey-veined pads of felt that spurted chalk – we pretended they were penises. She carried them out to the hockey pitch – there must have been dozens – and laid them in lines on the grass, so they read 'April Fool'. You had to laugh; you had to love, or at least admire Inez. Teachers seemed not to mind when her homework was late, or, if they did, she would shrug and care less. We quite often met in detention – bad girls, both of us, but I lacked her charm – where Inez would chitter with the sixth-former running the show. It was there that I learnt about periods, snogging, johnny bags, laxatives, soixante-neuf, VD clinics and what to do when uncles, fathers or dirty old doctors tried to touch you up. Inez and I never became friends. She moved with the fast set, but ahead, or aside slightly, even from them: vacations abroad, in hotels, with au pairs, not damp beds and cottages in Wales or the Dales, or a red-coated cabin along the south coast. A birthday treat for Inez, one year, was to see nude men in *Hair*: the whole class invited; parents aghast; ice cream in tubs, with lids that we licked, then flicked on the bare deal floor – we sat in the gods – and noisy Maltesers in red oblong boxes; chocolatey hands; crunching, greedy mouths; jealous green eyes. And brown ones that glowed – amber in the theatre, almost topaz in the neon lights; we walked through Chinatown and Soho, then zigzagged back through midnight frost to Eros, where we all linked arms, and were halfway up Regent Street, before someone bundled us into black cabs home; bellies and laps like heavy hot-water bottles, a soft damp palm on my warming neck. Not a couple of friends, plus Mum and Dad, anoraks and British Rail to Waterloo: *As You Like It* at the stuffy Old Vic; itchy seats, itchy feet; an aching, unyielding, long afternoon. In our O-level year, I, like many, acquired a boyfriend, a smoking habit and a tendency to truant. We all saw less of each other, more of the world, but Inez's world was wider and wilder than ours: she didn't need permission, she didn't need to lie, to see Lou Reed – on a Tuesday night – when he played at Shepherd's Bush; she was already hanging out with a bass guitarist, somewhere south of the river, inhabiting, not imagining, the dark side of the moon; Inez did speed and double lines of blue-white coke, while we smoked dubious hash in dank Acton bedrooms, with fluffy toys along the wall and horny, blurred boys, breathy on top of us, the curtains drawn. Inez and I kissed just once. Oh those sizzling z's and s's. That x. Witness: Mallory.

Mallory sat beside me in maths for five long years, she at the top, I at the bottom of the top division. She was clever and conscientious. I was lazy and not so clever. We were placed together for that very reason, in a desk for two, joined at the hip. Mallory had small eyes that focused, like darts, on the board, pinning those figures and giving them meaning, transcribing them – ever so neatly – on to the

45

squares of her dun-covered maths book. My eyes wandered. Mallory, folded next to me, was flat, stiff and long, her gym slip thin and hard as cardboard. She adhered to all the rules, wore regulation shoes even after we could choose. Why? Nothing rhymed. What did she eat for breakfast? I doodled a pair of platform boots and the outline of a Rice Krispies packet on the flowery jacket of my battered exercise book. What did her parents look like? Two stick people. Her house? Her bedroom? A single bed with a candlewick counterpane. I was good at beds; they were practice in perspective. Did Mallory have a boyfriend? No. Had she ever kissed? I did find that out. I drew two question marks, semi-joined, the first one back to front – a broken heart. Mallory resisted my probing, betraying only the flickiest signal of pain, with a slight retraction in the pupils of her eyes. Can I borrow your homework? Yes, with a sigh. Again. And again: Did she ever say 'fuck'? Did she even know what it meant? Was she a lezzy? Was I a bully? Was her pubic hair the same coarse texture as the peppery mane on her head, which was rough and dull, and hung un-adorned to her waist? When she bent her head to write, the swish of her hair brushed the summery down on my forearm, making it rise, separate, quiver. There was a knot in Mallory's hair, just behind and above the bulge of her ear. It never disappeared, that knot. Sometimes it altered in length, width or shape, but it never disappeared in five long years. Didn't she have a mother who cared, or someone other than me who noticed? And over those years, that poor knot, those long maths lessons and Mallory Beale became entwined in my mind as a kind of insoluble equation. I never got further than y times y equals y^2. Why, I could have counted the hairs on that girl's head, I knew her so well. Yet I couldn't work her out. Mallory let me copy her sums, but she wouldn't explain her workings. I was patient, though, and as my curiosity about Mallory increased, so did my respect, and respect, over five long years, grew slowly and surely to love. So when Mallory was witness to Inez and me, and that gold-set kiss, I wished she wasn't, because despite my inordinate love for her, I never kissed Mallory, not really, except in my dreams, in my head. I imagined it would be like kissing the dead. I was the prince, her hair was my forest, but I didn't hack it or tear at it, I didn't slice through the mess; I carefully lifted, twisted, unravelled the tangle, wetting the pink greasy skin around her ear with my spit, with my own, fat dart of a tongue. I kissed this princess on the lips, and her lips weren't ice or stone or noble marble, they were stringy skin, Mallory's own. No, I never kissed Mallory. But she kissed me, and then she kissed Yvonne instead.

Yvonne lived in a small terraced house just along from the school. Her mother – no father, no siblings – accompanied her to and from the old iron gates, from the age of eleven right through to sixteen. Everybody found this odd. Intriguing. Up to the age of eleven, Yvonne had lived in Switzerland. Or maybe Austria – I did find that out. Yvonne spoke German and was story-book pretty, with flaxen hair in two long plaits or a single, shorter, stubbier one. Her slow-blinking eyes were corn-dolly blue, and her nose and mouth were rosy hearts in the bigger heart of her face. She smiled a lot, but didn't say much. Milk-white teeth that later needed braces. Looking at her made me want to sniff her and eat her. She smelt of Omo, custard and snow. I wanted to bury my head in her like a dog, chase her like a bitch on heat, hunt, tryst, whelp, kill. But if I ate her, I wouldn't wolf her down, I would nibble her slowly, delicately – my alpine strawberry. For me, Yvonne was Heidi, obviously, and I

47

loved Heidi fantastically. But my love for Yvonne was a composite. Lotte and Lisa, Julie Andrews, the Chalet Girls: I superimposed them on Heidi-Yvonne. Because I could. Because I couldn't have loved her otherwise. Because Yvonne was a darling to look at, a picture in herself. But to look at only. If you actually came close, the fruit turned to poison, the snow to fire and those milk-white teeth to silver fangs. For Yvonne was a mean, secretive girl. A nasty piece of work. Ambitious by nature, pushed by her mother, Yvonne swotted like a demon, rising at dawn to practise the oboe, staying after school for extra elocution, and conjugating Latin verbs, humming them rhythmically under her breath – *amamus, amatis* – in between lessons. I was excited by and frightened of Yvonne. She had some very odd habits. Our classroom desks had lids that hinged, and on their undersides we pinned our timetables, gouged our initials, stuck our David Cassidys. Yvonne covered hers with sweet wrappers – cheap sweets, Black Jacks, Fruit Salads, Red Devils, penny chews. I never saw her eat them. In fact, I never saw her snack at all. But she ate the most enormous lunch, second helpings every day, and some days, if we were on first sitting, she would go in for the next sitting too. She had a lovely figure though – taut; all that skipping up mountains; dainty shins, bony knees, thighs that tapered and made an o at the top, like an open mouth. I imagined sticky fingers, slipping in, sweetness, then sour white froth. Yvonne knew all about kissing, French, German and more. Mallory's kiss was by no means her first. Her father was an army man, stationed in Wiesbaden. A bad man. He ought to be ashamed, Yvonne told Anna, who, being Anna, kissed her. Anna knew all about Yvonne.

Anna McKee, my very best friend. She died of cancer only last year. We'd bowled along together since the age of eleven; looks like I'll make half a century. We teamed up by chance: the alphabet, the zodiac, a girly desperation to be seen to have pals, and perhaps something else – a love at first sight. Anna was a sporty, bobbed-hair, blonde type of girl. A bit like me, but I'm a darker horse. Green-eyed and graceful, we both got good enough marks without really trying. Mostly we were on a par. Occasionally we sparred, but like good tennis partners, we improved each other's game. Metaphors mixed, syntax scrambled, we developed a private language, twisted our teenage histories into one. Equals, we thought, we doubled or multiplied the best in each other. We reflected. Our conceit. We were smart and we knew it. We looked good and felt good, arses together – in class, on the playing field, on dance floors; and, more memorably, on holiday: her caravan in Hastings – eager beavers from the sleazy town, page-boys and Wimpys, cod and chips and Babycham, windy kisses on the seafront, salt in our hair, and the vinegary afterwards; and the caravan afterwards. Or that B & B near Blakeney; we must have been thirteen; sneaking off in the pouring rain, catching a bus into Norwich, *Love Story* at the Gaumont, the nearly back row, damp ponchos, steaming, rehearsing; returning to a storm; nylon sheets that sparked and caught our toenails. At fourteen, we ambled and hostelled – the Lake District, Peak District, Hadrian's Wall – in clumpy boots and baggy shorts, carefully saved for, selected and practised in. Anna broke her boots in by walking fifty times, every evening all one spring, up and down her blossomy, lawny garden in Isleworth, with the river at the end of it, which made the grass wet and, as she wished, discoloured her tan leather boots, with the extra-long leather laces, tied round her ankles, twice; climbing behind her, I admired the neatness of the bows at the back, I admired the neatness of her ankles. I bought black pouchy monkey boots, with black waxed laces, and walked them in by stomping every day to school along the Great West Road, with cars powering down it even then from the new M4, Reading and Maidenhead. I scraped my boots along the pavement, deliberately scratching and scoring them. Between Anna's shorts and blue-flecked socks: brown legs, long legs, legs you wanted to suck because the beads on them glistened, the yellow hairs glittered and the thighs and the calves, the sinews and the muscles inside them heaved like deep water – bellows, a sough, the ripple of a promise. Later: Italian train compartments, Inter Rail, dawn ferries, Greek boys dancing, and Slavic girls singing *'Voulez-vous coucher avec moi, ce soir?'* Yes. Anna and I matched and were, we believed, a match for the world. What with lovers and travel, study and jobs, we went our healthy, separate ways for years, but we kept in touch – letters, phone calls, a drink or a meal – and then, when we found ourselves, quite by chance, neighbours again, in Wokingham, both married, with children, we re-buddied up – babycrap, kiddychat, the PTA – and settled down to a cruising, middle-of-the-road, achey sort of friendship. Anna's illness came on quickly. A routine smear. Precancerous lesions, probably harmless enough, but we'll do a biopsy, just to be sure. The biopsy showed level three dyskaryosis. She went for the chop – womb and ovaries, the whole bloody lot – but it wasn't enough. She stayed strong for the children, of course. She said it wasn't about being brave. She said she knew when she was beaten. But she was a good sport and would finish the game as one should, even though dying wasn't cricket. I watched her pack her hospital bag. When she'd packed for Europe a quarter of a century ago, she'd popped into her rucksack *La Nausée*, by Sartre, two halterneck bikinis and *The Second Sex* in chunky, orange Penguin translation. The books weren't read, but we bent their spines and made them look used, like our shoes, like passports. We shared the bikinis, burnt our backs, hoped for, expected and, in terms of promiscuous sex, undoubtedly got what we thought was the best of those halcyon, pill-safe, pre-disease-panicked days: the waiter in Zagreb, a barmaid in Split; Trieste station and the two dodgy brothers with the noisy old Vespa; Venice, Paris, the Bois de Boulogne. Don't go there, said Anna, zipping shut her flimsy bag. Yes, there's a link, but it's not divine retribution. God gave us contraception as well as cervical cancer. *Je ne regrette rien*, and you shouldn't either, *chérie*. She leant over, put her hand under the short, straight, now greying hair at the back of my neck, like she used to on buses and trains, in the caravan, at theatres, in cinemas, a midnight taxi; in dirty, smelly changing rooms, and on nameless Mediterranean beaches with turquoise seas that became transparent around our jiving bodies, our shuffled feet making little puffs of the yellow sand beneath. Then she pulled me forwards until our two heads touched. The prickle of hers made me shiver. She kissed me for the umpteenth time, on the forehead, the nose, my mouth. And much as I loved her, I wished the last kiss was from Inez.

1974 and all of us sixteen: an end-of-term treat, a field trip to Devon; exams in the bag, names in a hat – five to a tent, no argument. Inez, Mallory, Yvonne and Anna: my camp. Bluebells in seed and blackberries in flower, ragged robins, pink campion, cow parsley, teasels – urban girls in earthy lanes – only Mallory knew their names, those wild flowers. Mallory untied her tongue, rolled up her sleeves and taught us them, reciting Wordsworth, Keats and Shakespeare along the way. Why, I'll never know. Something in the Devon air? Something about digging a latrine together? Eating baked beans that we'd heated in billy cans – billy cans! – on an open fire? Or was it simply sharing a tent – the lumpy, caterpillar closeness, smelling of grass and plastic groundsheet, waking up with someone else's hair across your nostrils? The whole week was like that, full of surprises. The new head of sixth-form, whose idea it was to run the week, called it team-building. Ms Eliot was gay – I'm a lesbian, she said – and a feminist of course: she wore a bandanna, no bra and played the guitar. Ten Green Bottles, she jollied; Queenie was a lady; Oh, you'll never go to heaven. Was I a feminist? Were we happy? The very first night, Inez walked four miles to East Prawle, with the intention of phoning Papa and buying illicit scrumpy from the village shop. She returned with Tizer, wine gums and a pack of playing cards. That night in the tent, I expected her to teach us poker, to strip and gamble, but there we were at half past two, cross-legged on our sleeping bags, playing Snap and Happy Families, Beggar My Neighbour and Cheat, which made us giggle and wee, suck and fizz, until the torchlight dimmed, our eyes thickened, and if we hadn't slumped and slept, there would have been ghosts then girlish secrets in the air. It was a week to remember. We had little in the way of work and lots of time to ourselves and each other. We studied geology on Gara beach, then swam out to the granite rocks in the bay; Inez dived, Anna followed, the rest of us lolled – lizards, fish, seagulls. We studied erosion on the pink Lannacombe cliffs, then walked along them to the lighthouse at Start Point, where Anna and Yvonne had to piddle behind a tree because the lighthouse wasn't open to visitors on Tuesdays. The ruined village at shingly Hallsands, washed away in a terrible storm, decades ago, was a trysting place with bizarre acoustics. Ms Eliot introduced us to a trio of survivors, sisters who ran a hotel nearby. We were supposed to interview them, using portable tape-recorders. We preferred to record ourselves: Mallory mimicking Ms Eliot's nasal voice – I'm a lesbian, twanging around the derelict walls – and getting it right; Yvonne and myself duetting a flinty Queenie. Horses on Dartmoor and cream teas at a farm in South Allington, with cream that came from cows we'd seen milked: Yvonne with a scone, dripping strawberry jam, Anna and I spooning dollops of cream into each other's mouths, Inez and Mallory laughing, darting eyes and bubbling heads. The days it rained and we huddled in the tent all day, squashing flies, eating apples and damp, Digestive biscuits. The day the sun came out again. The day of the kissing. It was Kiss, Dare, Promise, Share that started things off. Mallory had to kiss me: stringy lips, keen mouth. She said it was her first kiss and she looked sad when it was over. Yvonne had to share: she told us about Wiesbaden and the bad things that happened there, and moving to Switzerland with her mother, and the bad things that happened there; then she cried, and Anna, being Anna, kissed her, tried to kiss things better; Mallory joined in, and Yvonne kissed back; then Mallory cried and said she was a lesbian and would we leave her alone for a while? Anna and Yvonne trotted off to find Ms Eliot, who had gone sailing in Salcombe with another group of girls. Inez and I strolled along the cliffs, not far. We waved to Mallory, who could see us from the camp all the time. The camp was in a hollow, with a stream that emptied into the sea. She waved back. You could see her poking at the small fire with a stick, then using bellows, arranging the pans on the top of it, stirring. You could hear, if you listened – snap, crackle, pop – but the land was still, and the smoke from the fire plaited smoothly up into air that was clear, with an evening chill. In front of us, there was a magnificent sunset. We stopped to admire it. The English Channel was chequered, pink and lilac, chopped with white and edged with blue-black patches under the shadow of the reddening cliffs. The sky zigzagged and rippled in shades of crimson, and the sun, sinking dizzily before us, was Penguin orange. So Inez and I kissed on the cliffs in the sunset. An image we all know well. It wasn't an extravagant, extrovert kiss, not really; more an experiment, a *joie de vivre* gesture, but perhaps something else – a sealing. It had been a good week. An age. What I recall, above all, isn't even the kiss, but the light in Inez's eyes, the way it changed, the way it burnt, the way it never died. Inez died within a couple of years of leaving school – run over by a rubbish van in Leicester Square. The details are squalid. High as a kite, the newspapers said. A French student, lying in the road – 3 a.m. – half-asleep. The rubbish van reversed over her. The driver simply didn't see her. There was a photo. It didn't look like Inez. As to the others, Yvonne, predictably, starved herself to death, and Mallory, less predictably, became a poet and threw herself under a train in New York. I forget which station.

These are the girls I loved. These are the girls who died. Inez, Mallory, Yvonne, Anna – *des jeunes filles en fleurs*.

GABI MacEWAN

Rise Above It

Eileen matthews first levitated at twenty-two minutes past three on a murky January afternoon. Her husband, Arthur, straining forward in his chair trying to coax a frayed shoelace through the eyelet of his battered brogue, did not witness the event. The first he realised that anything untoward had occurred was when Jasper the Yorkshire terrier, impatiently waiting for his constitutional, ceased to mimic shaking a rat to death with his lead and for the first time in his short life tried to howl.

It was an evil sound, not that it chilled the spine exactly – more that it set the teeth on edge in a most excruciating way. In his current position, hunched over the paunch he liked to believe he didn't carry, Arthur had no spare breath to mutter under, but he mentally cursed the day he had given in to Eileen's pleas for what she insisted on calling a 'Yorkie' to share their retirement flat. He would have preferred a more *manly* animal to be seen about with, a German shepherd perhaps or a Labrador, but the tenancy agreement stipulated one small pet and he would have had no excuse to get out of the place at all with a cat. Resentful but resigned, he raised his head to view the offending animal and then turned to follow its gaze.

Eileen had been 'resting her eyes' on the recliner their daughter and son-in-law had given them as a Christmas gift just two weeks before. Though sturdily built and covered in an inoffensive green velour, Arthur had taken a deep dislike to this piece of furniture as soon as he had tried it out. He had felt defenceless and undignified tipped back with his legs in the air like a stranded beetle and had clambered off straight away, loudly proclaiming that it would play hell with his sciatica. Considering how much time she spent in it now, Eileen had been quite tentative about taking her turn after that but finally she had been persuaded to sit and had been guided through operating the tilt mechanism until practically horizontal. Gingerly she had arranged her limbs in a posture of relaxation and closed her eyes. Almost immediately a rarely seen expression of bliss had spread across her face. It had been quite embarrassing to watch.

Mind you, it wasn't as alarming as what he was looking at now. For although Eileen's body was in much the same position as it had been when on the chair, it was now hovering eight or nine inches above it. Her pleated skirt hung down, just grazing the seat cushion, and from the angle Arthur was at, he had a view of rather more surgical support stocking top than he would like to see.

'Great Scott, woman, what are you doing?' he cried, abandoning the shoelace and launching himself to his feet.

His wife remained suspended in midair and now he was upright Arthur could see she wore the same silly smile as before. Arthur was frightened, not as rare an occurrence as he would prefer others to believe, but one that he tried to conceal with displays of other emotions.

'Eileen!' he shouted angrily, banging his hand on the sideboard for emphasis and to make himself heard above the horrible noises that continued to come from Jasper.

Her eyelids fluttered slightly and then, perhaps most disconcertingly of all, she floated back down to the recliner as gently and slowly as a dandelion tuft, not suddenly and with a bump as reason and gravity would expect she should do. The little dog quietened and went back to his lead but his master continued to stare.

Not pondering on life's upsets had always been one of Arthur's favourite maxims, and encouraging Eileen to adopt it a long-standing matrimonial chore. Anything that threatened her fragile emotional equilibrium, be it the shattering of a wedding present vase, the death of their first born – a son – in infancy, or a host of more inconsequential things, had thus been met with a terse 'Don't dwell, dear. Rise above it.' 'Dear' in this case was not so much a term of affection as a verbal tic, a habit that had grown over the years and which now also saved the embarrassment of having to fumble for a forename in ageing memory. Eileen used it too.

'I'm sorry, dear, I must have drifted off,' she said in her usual vague but pacifying way, rubbing her eyes and gazing up at her husband, not sure what command or criticism she might have missed this time. The unintended accuracy of her statement left Arthur at a loss as to how best to respond.

'I said I'm just taking young Jasper for his walk,' he lied and went out into the gathering dusk to prove it true with his shoelaces imperfectly threaded.

Maintaining a smart appearance was important to Arthur but uncharacteristically he gave this detail only the merest thought as, going against his own good advice, he was dwelling on the events of the preceding few minutes to some considerable degree. He walked around Hanover Gardens unaware of his surroundings or the direction he was taking, led unerringly by Jasper who trotted jauntily from lamppost to lamppost on the accustomed route and seemed to have quite forgotten his mistress's curious behaviour.

No one but fastidious Arthur would have spotted much wrong with his footwear anyway. The Turners at 7b, however, were standing at their lounge window with both curtains and floral nets drawn back to remove the flashing Santa attached to the glass. They watched him pass by in the gloom and noticed his usually rigid shoulders were slumped.

'He's looking old, Mavis,' said Mr Turner.

'Aren't we all, Reg?' responded his wife.

'Not you, my darling, you're as lovely as the day I married you,' said her husband.

'My darling' was definitely a term of endearment in the Turner household, and he took her in his arms for a kiss. Luckily Arthur's eyes remained fixed unseeing on the paving slabs ahead of him as he went past, for he hated public displays of affection even in the privacy of one's own home.

When man and dog returned from their walk everything was reassuringly normal. The tin lid of a Fray Bentos steak and kidney pie was on the work surface and Eileen was peeling away several layers of nutrition from some new potatoes to produce the uniform oval shapes her husband preferred. Arthur gave her a surreptitious sideways look. Her feet seemed to be planted firmly on the floor but he went over and pressed his hand on her shoulder to be sure. Surprised, she jumped and a slippery potato shot out of her fingers, bounced off the tap and landed in Jasper's food bowl where he was happily starting to devour his evening meal. Sticky brown reconstituted meat products splattered the cushion vinyl. He yelped and ran backwards, bumping into the clothes horse and entangling himself in several large damp white cotton undergarments. Arthur groaned and Eileen burst into tears.

'I only washed that floor this afternoon, and you know how it hurts my knees,' she whimpered, upset at the mess, but also, somewhat daringly, laying a little blame on Arthur for acting so strangely by touching her shoulder and causing the chaos to start.

'Don't dwell, dear. Rise above it,' muttered Arthur, scrabbling under the sink for a suitable cleaning cloth to hand her.

He was pleased to have something practical to do and that his world had apparently returned to its usual mildly irritating but comfortably mundane state.

A few nights later Arthur was drawn from the depths of slumber by finding himself cold in bed. Automatically he reached over his shoulder to retrieve some duvet from Eileen's grasp without bothering to open his eyes. But the duvet wasn't there and neither, apparently, was she. He flapped a questing hand behind him fruitlessly and then turned on to his back, peering into the darkness. Something large and pale was hovering above him. With an action that owed more to a recent season of adventure films on TV than his long-ago military training he threw himself sideways, landing awkwardly on the sheepskin-shaped rug. He struggled to his knees and then fumbled with the switch on the bedside light. Even then he couldn't be sure what it was he was seeing at first, it was too extraordinary to decipher. The pale shape was revealed to be the quilt in its pastel cover dangling unevenly from Eileen's body which hovered some three feet above the mattress.

Arthur swore loudly, something he wouldn't normally do in front of a woman but a sleeping one didn't count. Woken by the commotion, Jasper was yapping indignantly in the kitchen and Arthur, mortified, remembered how sound carried between the flats. All around them people were leading normal lives, trying to sleep peaceably in, not over, their beds.

Waiting for a moment or two until Jasper had grumbled into quietness again, he ordered, 'Eileen, come down from there!' in a hoarse stage whisper and then, for no explicable reason, turned out the light.

Temporarily night-blinded, he missed the descent but, hearing the softest rustle and creak of bedsprings, he knew she had once again floated back down to assume a conventional pose.

'Everything all right, dear?' she murmured, by the sound of it still half asleep.

'Just Jasper barking at something,' he answered, more truthfully than the first time, and warily climbed back into bed. Soon Eileen was wheezily snoring again but her husband, disturbed now in more ways than one, lay awake for the rest of the night.

The first incident had already caused Arthur a great deal of unease. He prided himself on being a rational man but try as he might he could not come up with any acceptable explanation for what he seemed to have seen. And yet he obviously had seen it because he wasn't the type to imagine things and that wretched dog had witnessed it too. Torn between lamely labelling it a trick of the light and simply pretending the incident had never happened, Arthur chose the latter. He'd grown quite adept over the years at blanking out occurrences he would rather not recall and had been managing quite successfully with this one too. Until now. Now all the puzzled thoughts were tumbling around in his brain again like washing in a dryer as the digital clock ticked away the seconds and the stars began to grow dim. When the boiler clicked into life, tired and troubled he reached for his dressing gown.

Arthur had always been an early riser. As a working man it had been a necessity but nowadays he simply appreciated the respite from Eileen's wittering on. In the kitchen he fed Jasper a handful of the dried dog food that looked like some other animal's droppings and made himself a large mug of coffee with three teaspoons each of Nescafé and sugar. Momentarily forgetting his current concerns, he grinned to himself as he enjoyed his daily act of nutritional rebellion. Eileen would have had a heart attack if she'd seen him, never mind warning him *he'd* have one!

But then he fell to seriously considering if she might really be unwell. His distaste and her discretion meant he knew very little about 'women's problems' but surely she'd been through the change a long time ago. What else could it be? For all her worrying he had to admit she was a remarkably healthy woman. A bit creaky around the joints perhaps and a tendency to chesty coughs but these hardly seemed to be relevant to the symptoms (if they were symptoms) she exhibited now.

For a few minutes he toyed with the idea that it might be something to do with her bowels, something that produced a strong and sustained burst of gas, but then he sighed and put his head in his hands. This was rubbish and he knew it and if there was any medical condition that caused sleeping people to float, doctors would induce it in the long-term sick and elderly to stop them getting bedsores. No, something else was at the root of these uprisings. He trawled through dim memories of Eileen's tedious accounts of her activities with the Hanover Ladies' Circle. There had been flower arranging – that had been how the vase got broken – and cake icing before Christmas but he couldn't remember anything unnatural, like séances or aromatherapy perhaps. So, putting the kettle on again to make Eileen her tea, he resolved once more not to dwell.

As time went by and the year grew older Arthur found Eileen in a state of levitation with increasing frequency until it settled down to around twice a week. Every three or four days (or nights) he would discover her doing what came naturally to no one, apparently, but her. Their lifestyle meant, mercifully, that no one else witnessed these events, but though Jasper became blasé about them Arthur found his own hallmark stoicism wearing somewhat thin. As for Eileen herself, she always stayed sound asleep throughout her upwardly mobile excursions and remained blissfully unaware that anything unusual was going on.

Since his retirement the couple were rarely far from each other's side for more than half an hour. But one morning when Arthur had been stuck in an interminable queue at the Post Office he had arrived home for his lunch a little late to find Eileen just launching off from the reclining chair. He had found this particularly disconcerting. What if he had been further delayed? He might have turned his ankle on a loose paving slab, for instance, and had to slowly hobble home in need of a compress. He might have been run over by a bus and been taken off to hospital for a stay of hours, days, weeks. He might never have come back at all and then where would Eileen be?

So long as he was always on hand to bring her back down to earth Arthur reasoned his wife could come to no harm. Yet precisely what the danger was he took such pains to protect her from he didn't care to imagine in too much detail. From that day forward, however, he hardly let Eileen out of his sight and encouraged her to come with him on his strolls with Jasper on the pretext of her needing more exercise. He even took to joining her in the lounge in the evening instead of returning to the kitchen table when she'd cleared away the supper things and spreading out the paper to meticulously read it from headline to sports page as had been his habit throughout their married life.

Eileen appeared happy enough with these new arrangements. She had never exhibited a great deal of self-sufficiency in Arthur's view so he thought she probably enjoyed the extra attention and company. Certainly she seemed a little calmer, a little more contented than before. And he didn't miss reading the paper as thoroughly as he used to. In the unlikely event of anyone mentioning the change in his behaviour he'd just say he needed new reading glasses but in truth he was finding it harder to concentrate recently. It was easier to let the far-fetched plots of the soap operas and detective series that Eileen favoured distract him from his nervous anticipation of their own improbable domestic dramas in the night to come. For although in her newly relaxed state his wife seemed to sleep even more easily, deeply and lengthily than before, Arthur nowadays only fitfully dozed, always on alert for some vertical movement beside him.

There was no one with whom he could share the burden of his bizarre knowledge. Certainly not Eileen herself. For one thing Arthur had never regarded his wife as a fully sentient being and wouldn't normally consult her opinion on a matter of such import, and for another putting an end to her ignorance of this particular issue would undoubtedly also bring to an end the mellowness she'd shown of late. If the situation was distressing him God alone knew what it might do to her.

Always so self-sufficient himself, Arthur had never been one to court or encourage emotional bonds. Apart from

Eileen's recent forays to the local community centre the Matthewses' social interaction largely consisted of passing the time of day with their neighbours and exchanging greetings cards with a few distant surviving kin. Now, too late in life for it to be of any use, he realised what friends were for. Hard though it was to swallow his pride, he knew he had to talk to someone, and soon. He needed a helping hand or at least a listening ear but who could he ask to lend it?

The only possible candidate for confidante was their daughter Susan, an alarmingly large and loud woman who made the china ornaments rattle when she entered their home. Tim, her husband, who might have been a more likely choice on grounds of his potentially superior masculine mind, seemed so ineffectual and effeminate next to his strident spouse that he never really entered the running at all. So Susan it had to be. They were due for a visit the coming Easter weekend and Arthur decided to broach the subject then.

The weather was unseasonably warm on the Sunday. Eileen fretted a little about her new sandals rubbing a corn and the possibility of the chicken becoming a health hazard before it defrosted enough to cook. Arthur was pleased he'd kept certain things to himself so far. Compared to the frantic way she'd prepared for their occasional guests in the past this was insouciance indeed. Then late morning the visitors arrived. The couples gave each other over-wrapped and over-priced confectionery items appropriate to the day and Arthur attempted to engage the monosyllabic Tim in conversation about what route he'd taken to drive there while Susan and her mother served the meal.

When Eileen went into the kitchen to wash up the lunch things Tim accompanied her to dry. Arthur had always taken a dim view of men who helped with domestic chores but now was his chance. Gruffly and without preamble as was his way, he turned to his daughter and blurted out *sotto voce*, 'I'm worried about your mother.'

Susan raised a quizzical eyebrow. That there had been some fundamental changes in the parental home had not escaped her. Her father's physical deterioration since Christmas was shocking. He had lost weight, his skin had developed a greyish hue and he was in constant minor motion, twitching and fidgeting all the while especially when the woman he'd tried for years to ignore or evade was out of the room for a minute or two. Her mother on the other hand positively glowed. If she'd been younger you might have thought she was pregnant, or having an affair. Susan grimaced. There were things she didn't want to imagine in too much detail either. She was as forthright as her father, she cut to the chase.

'You need to see the doctor, Dad,' she told him.

In bed that night Arthur considered this suggestion. He ran through several possible scenarios in his head. At least he tried to produce different predictions of events but they always ended up much the same. The GP would open with an amiable 'Now what seems to be the trouble?' or some such enquiry, Arthur would describe what was happening to his wife and then the doctor would examine *him*.

The heat of the day had continued into the darkness almost unabated. As Eileen had requested the window be left a little ajar to ease the tightness in her chest, the sounds of drunken whoops and yells, car horns and police sirens kept sabotaging Arthur's attempts to stop thinking and join his wife in dreams. Perhaps a cup of Ovaltine might help, he wondered wearily. Sighing, he got up and, bribing Jasper back into his basket with a biscuit or two, quietly made his drink and went to sit in the lounge.

65

The room was dimly lit by the glow of the streetlamps outside and a chink in the curtains cast a streak of orange spotlight on the recliner. Arthur eyed it suspiciously, mug in hand. It seemed such an innocent piece of furniture but what trouble it had brought about! Yet despite his accusations, and initial misgivings as to just how relaxing reclining could be, it did look rather inviting now. With no one around to witness his vulnerability it offered a safe haven of comfortable repose. Glancing furtively about him, he eased himself on to the seat and tilted his body back.

For the first time in several months Arthur fell into a long deep sleep. When he awoke the room was bright and stifling and Jasper was whining and scratching at the kitchen door. Alarmed by the apparent lateness, Arthur ignored his canine pleas and strode first the few paces to the bedroom. The duvet was flung back almost to the floor, revealing slight indentations in the mattress and pillow from Eileen's substantial form but no sign of the woman who had made them.

He hoped she was in the bathroom collecting towels to add to the bed linen for the Monday morning wash. He hoped with the fervent futile hope of the unbeliever's prayer, knocking on the door before turning the handle to demonstrate his faith. Eileen wasn't there. Neither was she in the kitchen/diner, the lounge he had just left or the cupboard in the hall.

A lesser man might have panicked but Arthur knew the internal commotion he could feel was only indigestion, his breathlessness merely caused by rushing about. Back in the bedroom, pretending to himself he was going to get dressed and look for his absent wife, he watched the curtains flap for a while before bravely pulling them apart. The window, as he had known all along it would be, was as wide open as it would go. Even so it must have been a bit of a squeeze. A fragment of pink brushed-nylon nightie clung to the latch. He steeled himself to look down at the communal gardens but there was no tangle of twisted limbs, not even a flattened shrub to show she had landed beneath.

A few streets away the town hall clock chimed the quarter hour. Arthur turned to see its familiar illuminated face and despite his distraction noticed something odd about the minute hand which seemed to have a more ornate and curvaceous shape than he remembered. Then, long-distance vision still remarkably acute, he realised it was the silhouette of Eileen that he could see, horizontal and high in the morning air, passing between the nine and the three. As he watched she cleared the clock face and began to travel at some considerable speed towards the open sky.

JANEY HUBER

The Serpent's Child

T HE SALESGIRL wonders why we're together. Why is this chic white woman with fox cub hair accompanied by a huge, gawky black girl? Her eyes slide over me and shut me out: I must be a servant, or an object of charity. She focuses on my companion, calculating her worth: the apricot wool suit with its big buttons (is it Chanel?), the Hermès scarf, the clam-shell bag.

'*Je peux vous aider, Madame?*'

'*Oui, Mademoiselle. Je cherche des chaussures pour ma fille.*'

A tremor crosses the salegirl's face, a twitch of the eyebrows, a quiver of the mouth. Can I be this woman's daughter? she wonders.

My mother points out the shoes she wants for me. They are a scaly black leather, like crocodile. I will wear them to her funeral.

I parade back and forth in the too-small shoes. Her face settles into its usual expression, puzzled but determined: she will remake this dark, ungainly daughter in her own image.

'Good, we'll take them,' she instructs the salesgirl.

I let my back slump into its usual question mark, and sit down beside my mother to remove the shoes. I loom over her. My shoulders spread out over the armrests, my knees project out from the seat. I tuck my feet under it to conceal their size.

My mother is petite, feminine, sherry-coloured. Her hair is like stem ginger in syrup, her eyes are bright caramels, fringed by thick pale lashes. She reminds me of a hamster: she has big front teeth and a short upper lip which tugs on her nose when she speaks, making it twitch. Nobody else notices this; men in particular find her eager, girlish.

I am an embarrassment to her with my wide bony face, my dark skin. I trail around behind her like a grotesque shadow. I am surprised she had me at all – perhaps she is more of a Catholic than she appears.

I take after my father.

'That worm,' my mother says. 'Pushing off as soon as I got pregnant. He didn't even leave an address.'

He was attached to the Nigerian consulate, or so he said, one of the flotsam and jetsam of the world that comes to rest in this city, Geneva, before floating off on the next tide. She met him at the park near her work, where she sat nibbling a cheese roll in the June sunshine. He was as long and slender as an ebony cane, smartly dressed, almost effete. She was not afraid of him, though she had just come from Ireland, and was at sea in this cosmopolitan world, taking dictation about trade agreements between countries that she could hardly find on the map, let alone spell. He was courtly, and gentle, and returned every lunch time for a week to meet her on the park bench, before inviting her out to dinner.

She supposes now that she was easy prey. She felt so glamorous, drinking Martinis in the glittering bar of the Hôtel du Rhône, being served three different wines at dinner.

'I remember seeing his black hand holding my white one on the linen tablecloth, like yang and yin, two opposite

70

halves making a perfect whole. But he didn't see it that way. . . . Well, you were the result. When I told him, he disappeared off the face of the earth.'

She went to the Nigerian consulate – they had never heard of him. Had he given her a false name? But he had given her a real child, a ten-pound changeling that grew into her enormous daughter.

'You split me open like a chestnut coming out of its shell,' she said. 'My whole womb was pulled out! They had to chop it off. But perhaps it's as well; having kids is so bad for the figure.'

Can it be true? I picture the bloody inverted caul of her uterus, like the membranous egg of a reptile, beside my blood-smeared newborn body. Was I born with such violence? I should have given birth to her – her tiny body would fit easily into mine, and she would be born neatly, with her little paws folded before her, her pointed chin resting on them.

Why didn't she go back to Ireland?

'Are you mad? My father would have beaten me black and blue. He had a hard hand.'

I met her father once, before he died, when he reluctantly came to see his daughter, as she would not come to him. He was a wide-necked countryman with suspicious eyes, and a thin tongue that flickered in and out of his mouth, as if tasting the air for danger or prey. His palm was dry and calloused. I could imagine it leaving violet bruises liquefying under his daughter's suede skin. His wife scurried along beside him, humble and mute, hoping to remain unnoticed. They were not interested in me: my mother had told them I was adopted.

'And to have the whole street gossiping, and my sisters laughing behind my back?' she went on. 'No, thank you. Anyway, there was a very good crèche at work.'

71

I have seen the place she worked then – the polished marble entrance hall, the teak panels from Indonesia, the hushed conference chamber with its interpreters' booths and jacks for headphones. Why would she leave it, to return to the pub, the shop, the church? I am glad she didn't. I would have been an even stranger creature there, among the paper-skinned women of her family, with their red squirrel hair. At least in this city I am among my own, the exiled, the dispossessed, the expatriate. We weave in and out among the stocky sallow natives, our eyes lowered to avoid re-cognition, our mouths closed over our alien tongues. We are like secret agents: we know much of them, they know little of us.

My mother leads me towards the dress department.

'What about this one?' she asks, holding out a size twelve dress from the rack.

'Mother, you know black doesn't suit me.'

'It's a classic look, Sarah dear. Try it on.'

Sarah. A name between a hiss and a sigh. I wish I had been called Bathsheba, or Ayesha, or one of the rhythmical, tripping names from my father's country, which sound like the knocking of drums. He was called Mohammed – should I be Muslim? I have bought a silver Hand of Fatima at a stall, and I wear it inside my clothes, to bring me good luck. I see it now as I take off my blouse, shimmering against my dark skin, beside the little gold cross my mother gave me.

I ease the new dress over my hips. I have to breathe out to do up the zip – it feels like a corset. The black linen makes my skin look yellow-brown, eczematous. Does my mother not see me as I am? She chooses colours and styles that would suit a small white woman. Or does she wish me to be plain, a sullen dark backdrop to her own honeyed bright-ness? I go out to present myself.

'Perfect,' my mother says. 'You can wear that to Mass.'

We attend church now, but I am cynical: I think my mother hopes to find another husband there. Her faith is cyclical, convenient. She had me baptised out of habit, then sent me to the Catholic school where I could be educated well and cheaply. She did not hesitate to marry a Protestant when one became available.

My first glimpse of Per was when I was three. He looked like an icicle, with his transparent skin and straight back. He bent in the middle to speak to me, carefully attentive, accepting my existence with Swedish pragmatism. When they were married, we made an exotic trio: the glacial father, the treacle mother, the charcoal child. A trio typical of this city.

This city. This tapestry of nations, this shifting fabric, like a curtain of beads, rippling and twinkling, never static. My mother came into it as a chip of orange plastic; now she is a polished amber gem. She was a common goldfish; now she is as sleek and exclusive as a Koi carp. Has she left her past behind? I see her kneeling at Mass, taking the Host on her pink tongue, and swallowing it with her eyes shut, and I wonder: perhaps the small-town Irish girl is still there, still hoping for absolution.

Her sins seem little to me: an illegitimate child, a divorce. She has a shallow nature, a desire to remain young. Are these so wrong? My only regret is the impact they have had on me. I have been an impediment to her.

Per left us when I was thirteen, four years ago. It was a wise decision, though my mother didn't understand it.

'Why, Per?' she said plaintively. 'We were so happy.'

And we were happy, when I was a doll in white dresses, with red ribbons in my hair; when Per could bounce me on his lap, my little fists waving like ripe blackberries against his ivory shirt; when he could steady the bicycle as I wobbled along, my legs like the stalks of winter saplings against the chalk dust road. Do I just remember the photographs? The ones with me in them all look like negatives.

I loved Per as my father. I felt as luminous and bright as he. When I oiled my skin until it shone I felt like a dark sun, glowing beside his pure Nordic light, a perfect foil for him. He was fond, and kind. I never thought he would leave us.

Then, at twelve, my skin began to feel too tight for me, and my buttocks swelled into tense globes almost overnight, bringing out stretch marks like silver snail tracks on my skin. My breasts punched out like fists, and the innocuous coffee discs that topped them became as solid and dark as blood-filled thumbs, poking out of my shirt. I felt like one of the speeded-up films in biology class, where flowers unfolded and shot up from seeds, then swelled into fruit, and burst their leather cases to shake themselves out over the land. I was like that also: abundant, generous, fecund.

I had been accustomed to running about the house naked as a child, as free as a little pony, my pink secrets concealed under dark pads of flesh. I was a different species from the adults, there was no risk of cross-breeding. Then, as I unfurled, became female, my mother cautioned me to modesty. I was to wear a bathrobe, to hide myself.

She went to a bridge party one night, and I decided to have a bath.

Per was downstairs watching television. I soaked in musk-scented oil, smoothing its viscous beads into my skin until it was supple and gleaming. I felt languid, indolent. I rose and shook myself dry, not wanting to rub off the oil, and pulled out the plug. The water rushed noisily down the pipes, signalling the end of my bath.

74

I admired myself in the bathroom mirror: the nipples like candied violets, breasts like chocolate fairy cakes, glistening with sugar drops. I couldn't help comparing myself to my mother: her breasts were like rolls of lumpy batter, which slid down her ribs when she removed the artificial cones of her bra. I ran my hands over my hips, rubbing in the oil, then, forgetting my bathrobe, I stepped out on to the landing.

Per was there. Was he waiting for me? Surely not – he had a book in his hand, he was on his way to the study. But he stood, immobile, and looked at me.

I should have turned back, or hurried on. But I also stood, brazen, and let him look.

His frosty skin began to change, as if a volcano erupted beneath it. The hot blood coursed upwards and distended the crust of his face, boiled into his lips to make them lava pipes, pressed forward behind his eyes until they became reddened and engorged like the eyes of a dragon.

I watched him, amazed.

Then he slapped me.

A hard blow to my cheek, hard enough to knock me against the door frame, delivered with an agonised grunt. He hurried down the stairs, grabbed his jacket, and rushed out, slamming the door behind him.

I lay on the carpet, its rough loops scratching my cheek. I did not weep. It was what I deserved.

I pretended to be asleep when my mother came home. Per came back later. I heard him in the study, leafing through papers as the night wore on. In the morning he went out early, before I came down for breakfast. I could see the dark marks of his fingers on my cheek, like the charred striations on grilled meat, but my mother noticed nothing. Her concern was for Per.

'He's got an important meeting today – something about steel subsidies. He won't be back till late. Shall we have supper in front of a video?'

My mother is a chatterer. She didn't notice that I made no reply, that I hunched beside her, my arms over my chest, my head hanging. Several days passed, in which she twittered and preened as usual before she noticed the chill that had crept into the house; the polite reserve between Per and me.

'Your father's tired,' she explained. 'He's under a lot of pressure.'

I heard him fidgeting downstairs at night. I heard him making love to my mother, the thud of the bedsprings, her little squeals. I blushed for him.

He began to travel more. Ours was a city of travellers, a no-man's-land of wives and children making do while fathers were in Africa or in India, a transit lounge where they touched down for refreshments before the next leg of their journey. Per had resisted this in the past – now he threw himself into it. My mother began to moult, letting grey show in her terracotta hair, ignoring the chips in her tangerine nail varnish. A button fell off her coat and she didn't replace it. She forgot to polish her shoes.

'I think he's having an affair,' she confided tearfully one night as we sat together on the sofa, on our own again. 'Why else would he be away so much? Your father didn't want me; now Per doesn't either.'

He duly confessed some infidelity, but I knew the truth. I lay in bed at night, imagining his white hand searing my dark thigh, and was ashamed. I yearned to escape the sad house, to roam at will through the city, which lay coiled on its nest at the base of the mountains, blinking and watchful in the dark. Instead, I lay sweating and restless in my tangled sheets, my skin itching and chafing. Then the fever

76

subsided, and I became passive; obedient to my mother's commands; slothful in my cold solitude.

In the four years since he left us, my mother has recovered. Her concern for her looks has returned; her skin is once again fine-grained and uniform with foundation, her hair a russet toque. In the absence of a husband she has turned her attention to me, trying with irritable affection to make me less big, less black, less gauche. It is a project doomed to failure.

Now, as the new dress is wrapped, she is weary.

'I feel a bit peculiar, darling. Shall we have a cup of tea somewhere?'

Smudged crescents like dirty thumbprints have appeared under her eyes. She leans on my arm and I take her to the tea room on the second floor. She takes little bites of her carrot cake – she has no appetite.

'I think I need a lie down.'

I take her home. She gestures at the bags – I am to put them away. I hang the black dress in my wardrobe while she gets into bed, then I take her another cup of tea. She is in her blouse and tights under the blankets.

'Let me help you with your jewellery.'

I undo the chunky gold necklace, slip the opal ring off her finger. It comes off too easily. The bones of her hand are like tent poles from which the skin hangs, a greenish fabric. She still smells of Shalimar, of cold cream, but I think there may be something rotting underneath.

Within days she lies in a hospital bed, held in the bracket of the white sheets like a tennis racket. The game is over.

I stay alone at home, preoccupied by the vision of her flesh dissolving away. I eat obsessively, swallowing lumps of cheese while standing at the fridge door, running to the corner shop for chocolate bars which I tear open and eat on

77

the pavement, cooking massive bowls of spaghetti and frying the leftovers for breakfast.

These do not satisfy me. I cook roasts and chops and bacon, salivating as the blood rises to the surface in the pan, tearing off great chunks with my teeth before they reach the plate, gorging until I am satiated, then lying distended and quiescent on the sofa until I fall asleep.

She continues to shrivel. Soon she is no more than golden fluff over small brittle bones, though she is still vain: her hair is as carefully sculpted as a wig on her skull. Her skin clings to her jaw and cheekbones like cellophane – the cancer has consumed all the fat between the two. At least she no longer has to diet, I think, and am startled by my unkindness.

On the morning of her death I sit beside the knitting needle body with its slack work of skin, watching her fingers pluck at invisible specks on the sheet. She becomes aware of me, peering up with drug-hazed eyes like crystal-lised fruits.

'Will you help me with my nails, dear?'

I shake the bottle of coral nail varnish; the pear-drop smell cuts the sweet faecal odour that floats over the under-lying wash of Ajax. I hold her hand: each finger is like a wax taper, stiff and fragile. The varnish lights a flame of colour at the tip of each, a shocking bloom on dry relics.

'I like to look my best,' she sighs, and shuts her eyes.

Those were her last words to me.

I wear the black dress to church, as she intended. I can barely do it up now. I have to push the folds of flesh away from the zip, before it clicks up sleeper by sleeper, a train uniting the cloth fields on either side. When it reaches the top I hardly dare breathe. I cram my feet into the black

78

shoes she bought me. They will only be comfortable if I chop off my toes.

The funeral service is in the soot-stained Catholic church, in the poorer part of this Protestant city, among the dilapidated apartment blocks where the Italian immigrants live. She would not be buried in Ireland, and her lawyers have respected her wishes. Her sisters are here, resentful and muttering; they overlook me. I have devised a reading which neither they nor the priest will like. I deliver it anyway, breathing carefully in my tight dress, looking out over the assembled women in their dark colours. There are a few men, husbands of her sisters and friends, but Per is not here – he lives in Sweden now. I miss him suddenly, painfully – my connection with him is broken this day.

'The Lord God said to the woman, "What have you done?" And the woman said, "The serpent tempted me, and I did eat." And the Lord God said to the serpent, "I will put enmity between you and the woman, and between your seed and her seed. She shall bruise your head, and you shall bruise her heel." And there was war in heaven, and the dragon was cast out into the earth, and went to make war on the remnant of her seed.'

There is an uneasy rustle of movement as I sit down, but the priest takes over with calm professionalism. My thoughts return to Per. Over the years the image of his hand has changed – the white heat of it, branding my thigh, has become a cool red. Now it becomes my own palm, dipped in henna, prepared for the burning grounds. I want to burst into flames on his pyre, to be a glowing sun again, immolated for him. I put my head in my hands.

The service comes to an end. My mother's sisters have prepared funeral sweetmeats in the church hall, dispensing with an Irish wake in this unfamiliar setting. Her friends

79

dab their eyes with hankies then lunge for the petits fours and coffee. I leave them to it, and make my way out to the car park.

I feel a terrible surge of rage as I stand there alone. I take a deep breath, and my dress splits down the front with a harsh crack. I look down, and see the gorgeous scarlet lozenge of my slip revealed, like a new skin. I stretch my feet and my shoes give way at the seams. I slough them off into the gutter.

I can breathe now, and stand straight. My anger still flows out from my core to my fingertips, and I tear off my cross and the Hand of Fatima and throw them into the bushes. I have no use for them.

The city's lair awaits me. I move down the street, monstrous, undulant, incandescent.

For I am the child of dragons, and my time has come.

KATE PULLINGER

In Lieu of Parenting

MY THERAPIST was following me.

I'd been seeing her for so long I'd almost forgotten I was seeing a therapist. I thought of her as part of my routine, like taking a bath or going to the barber. I'm not actually interested in therapy; I don't have much faith in it. But my father pays for me to go in lieu of parenting. So I go. I don't say much – what is there to say after all these years? She knows almost everything there is to know about my childhood and, frankly, my childhood is not that interesting: I was born, I grew, my parents made me miserable. After that I left home, met my wife, had my son, and discovered how to be happy. But still, I went along and I sat on her couch. It felt like too much of a cliché to lie down, so I remained upright. I spent quite a lot of the time – time I imagine she thought I was mulling over what to say next – trying to figure out how to get the money my father paid her for myself, but as he sent a monthly cheque, and I didn't even know what her hourly rate was, I didn't make much headway.

At the time, my therapist was undergoing some kind of training. She told me about it – now that was a surprise, my therapist telling *me* things. I'd never really got used to it, even though it happened frequently. Although I wasn't interested in therapy, or in therapists, I'd watched enough

TV to have an idea of what it should be like and I had always imagined she would remain largely silent, just asking the odd question to get me started on the fascinating story of my own life (or not, but you see what I mean) or making a pithy but thought-provoking comment once every couple of years. But, in fact, she was talkative. Some days I'd pretend that I was the therapist and she was my patient and while she talked, I'd nod sagely. Other days I'd pretend that I was Tony Soprano and she was Dr Melfi but I couldn't dwell on that particular scenario for too long because, truth be told, like Tony Soprano, I fancy Dr Melfi. And from time to time I'd imagine that I was John Cusack in *Grosse Pointe Blank*, a hit man racked with neurosis, and that my therapist was, in fact, very very frightened of me. But mostly I just sat there with a kind of stupid blank look on my face and we alternated between silence and the therapist telling me stories about her latest bout of training.

She was always training! It was as though herself-as-therapist was in a state of continual evolution, continual revolution; she was always learning new things. I suppose if I'd been interested in therapy, my own or anyone else's for that matter, this could have been fascinating. But, I'm sad to admit, I did not pay much attention to the things my therapist had to say to me.

But a few things filtered through anyway. For example, I knew that recently she'd been studying someone called Hillman or Hillsman and that Hillman had some kind of theory of psychotherapy that involved getting to know the patient beyond the confines of the therapy room, moving with the patient out in the world once the session had finished, getting on the tube train with them. I remember thinking at the time that this bit, the getting-on-the-tube-train-with-your-patient bit, must have been a metaphor for a particularly patient-centred approach to therapy, but it seems not, or at least not as far as my therapist was concerned; this was something to interpret literally. I don't know. All I do know for sure is that my therapist started following me.

The first time it happened I thought it was a coincidence. I'd never run into my therapist in London before, but in a way that wasn't surprising; I don't live anywhere near her practice and London is a very big city. I was in the West End, doing a bit of shopping in John Lewis. I like to look in on the kitchen department from time to time; I'm interested in coffee grinders and colanders and Le Creuset. These are the things that make me feel real in life, they make me feel I can say, look, here I am, I am a grown-up person, I'm buying tongs, I'm a married man with a kitchen and a wife and a child.

I caught sight of her across the shop floor. She was looking straight at me. She blanched – I saw her blanch, it was unmistakable, I probably blanched right back at her – and then she ducked down behind the row of KitchenAid blenders, one of which I would be able to afford if I could ever figure out how to get my hands on the money my father forked out every week for my therapy. I wasn't surprised that she didn't want me to see her, so I paid for the toaster tongs and went on my merry way.

During the next session I thought about asking her about our chance meeting – although you could hardly call our chance passing a meeting – but I didn't want to embarrass her, and I didn't want to remind her that we'd breached the etiquette of the therapy session in this tiny but potentially damaging way. Imagine if I had been interested in therapy; imagine if I'd been experiencing a

83

bit of transference or something like that, that well-documented (in the movies and on TV at least) phenomenon when the patient falls a little bit in love with the therapist. Or maybe a lot of love. Obsessed. Wants to actually possess the therapist, have sex with the therapist, spend the rest of his or her life with the therapist. This happens, apparently. Not to me, of course, as I wasn't interested in therapy and, consequently, wasn't interested in my therapist either. So I didn't say anything.

But then it happened again. On Monday of the following week I was in HMV browsing the CD racks, thinking about how in another minute or two CDs might become entirely obsolete, and wondering if anyone would mourn the passing of the CD in the way that many people mourned, and continue to mourn, the passing of the vinyl LP. I was in Americana and there she was, over in R&B. She was standing there, and she was staring at me. I saw her, she saw me see her, she blanched, as usual, and then, believe it or not, she ducked down behind the row of CD racks. This time I couldn't help myself and I went after her, but she was gone. She was nowhere to be seen. She must have remained bent over double and walked as quickly as possible straight out the front doors of HMV.

Two days later, in the ladies' scarf department on the ground floor of Liberty, where I was thinking about a birthday present for my wife, there she was. My therapist. Staring at me.

I go into the West End all the time. I pass through on the way home from work and I often get off the bus and go for a wander in the shops, though I hardly ever buy anything; even if I linger over the saucepans I can still get home in time to be there when my boy gets back from school. I have no idea what draws me there, it's not as though the West End of London is all that wonderful – it's very crowded for one thing, and the shops are mainly enormous versions of the same shops you find in every other high street – but there is something about it that I like, something that comforts me. It's a widely known fact that the centre of London has more CCTV cameras than anywhere else on earth, that as you move from shop to shop you are under surveillance every step of the way. I've heard it said that the only place you aren't filmed is in the John Lewis toilets.

But now, every time I got off the bus, no matter where I went, no matter how zigzaggy or nonsensical a route I took to get there – the chemist, the sock department of a big department store, the expensive shops off in the side streets – my therapist would somehow find me. Two, maybe three times, each week. I kept going to see her and, because I hadn't mentioned it the first time, it felt silly to mention it the second time, and then it would have seemed odd to mention it when it had happened three times and was clearly not some kind of weird and wonderful coincidence, fate throwing me and my therapist together with unnerving determination. I sat opposite my therapist, and I looked around the cosy room with its proliferation of cushions and books and lamps that threw out a warm orange light, and I looked at her – neither of us were talking at that point, she was writing in her notebook – and I realised that my therapist was stalking me.

What could I do? I couldn't stop going to see her, that was out of the question. Firstly, if I stopped going to see her, I'd never have the chance to figure out how to get the money my father paid her every month diverted into my own pocket. Secondly, I didn't want to tell my father that I'd stopped seeing the therapist, mainly because that would mean I'd actually have to ring him up and speak to him, something we'd both been avoiding for a very long time indeed. Thirdly, I'd no longer be pretending that my therapist wasn't following me, so she'd definitely know that I knew she was following me, and God knows what she'd do then – she'd probably have to kill me.

But, I reasoned as I sat there opposite my therapist who had started to follow me several weeks previously, if she tracked me down in the West End and tried to kill me, at least it would be on CCTV. There'd be plenty of witnesses because it's always so crowded and that would make it easy for the police to track down the tape that contained footage of the murder – blurry, pixellated, but sufficiently detailed to be used in court. From that day onward I made sure never to go to the loo on my way home, never to end up alone in the men's toilets in John Lewis. Which meant that most nights I walked in the front door of the house bursting for a wee.

I was going to have to tell my wife what was happening.

My wife and I are very happily married. We've been married for a long time and we live together in a state of permanent tranquillity. She's the main breadwinner, and I'm the main parent, and these roles suit us both perfectly. That's not to say we haven't had our ups and downs, because we have. There was that problem I had with the Mormons the year before. She knew all about that. They kept coming to my door and trying to make me their leader. They said I was calling to them through the ether. Each time they knocked I opened the door and remained polite, as did they. After a few months of unflagging politeness, they stopped coming. I knew they were disappointed in me – a leader refusing to lead – but there was nothing I could do about it; I'm an atheist, for heaven's sake. I was relieved when they stopped, but, to tell the truth, I also missed them a little. My wife was understanding throughout the whole episode – though, of course, she was never home when the Mormons came by – and she said she hoped I would talk about it with my therapist. I didn't, of course, but I didn't tell my wife that either; it is these small untruths that perpetuate tranquillity.

But I felt compelled to tell her that my therapist was following me. We were sitting together, watching the telly.

'She's what?'

'I know it sounds strange, but a couple of times a week . . .'

She cut me off. 'How many times exactly?'

'Well,' I said, reluctant to admit it, 'I've spotted her a dozen times now, spread over the past five or six weeks.'

'A dozen times?!'

'I know. Weird, isn't it?'

'Are you sure it's her?'

I crossed my arms and gave my wife a look. The boy was in bed, fast asleep; he was very good at falling asleep, it was one of the many things I admired about him and the way he lived his life.

My wife continued to speak. 'I don't know what to say.'

'She must be in love with me, don't you think?' My tone was conspiratorial; I thought my wife and I could have a little laugh about this strange situation.

'In love with you?'

'Reverse transference, or something.'

My wife did laugh then. 'You should report her.'

'To whom?'

'I don't know.'

We both fell silent, contemplating.

'I'm thinking about stopping,' I said.

'Stopping what?'

'Going to see her.'

'Really?'

'It seems like madness to continue – I mean, clearly she's the one with the problem, not me.'

'I don't know, honey.'

'What?'

'Maybe you need that therapy.'

I know that my wife doesn't believe that my therapist is following me. She didn't really believe that the Mormons were trying to make me their leader either. But she humours me, which is sweet of her; it is what is required for perpetual tranquillity.

We kept the boy out of all of this, of course. He's just a boy, interested in football and collecting incredibly expensive trading cards and negotiating to be allowed to watch the same things his friends are allowed to watch on telly. He's not interested in therapy or my therapist; in fact, it's safe to say he's even less interested in my therapist than I am. During the day he goes to school and at night he sleeps soundly. My wife and I went back to watching telly.

And then it stopped. As suddenly as she began, my therapist stopped following me. Several days went by before I realised I hadn't seen her in any of the shops for a while, then a whole week passed. I waited another week before I risked saying anything and then, of course, I didn't want to say anything too direct or incriminating. So what I said was this:

'I'm thinking about getting in touch with my father.'

Her response was gratifying: her eyes went very wide with surprise and amazement, although, for once, she didn't actually say anything.

'I'm thinking about giving him a ring.'

KATHRYN SIMMONDS

Pentecost

I T WAS early June, the second week after Pentecost and the second week of the heatwave. Jerome was standing in the garden centre staring at a row of seedlings, now and again weighing a stem between his fingers, studying the tiny photos to see how the plants would eventually look. His body still felt clammy, even though he was wearing his lightest clothes – linen trousers and a white cotton shirt. The experienced gardeners made their way around him; an old man with a face the colour of terracotta; a young red-haired woman, her trolley overflowing with shrubs. He thought of phoning his mother. In the end he picked up a tray and headed for an alcove of potted ferns where it was cool.

Whenever Jerome pictured his mother she was in the garden. As a child he'd come home from school to find her there; shifting her sunhat with the back of her wrist, she'd exclaim, 'Darling!' as if she hadn't seen him for a week. According to the family story, a lady in a department store had once crouched to ask Jerome his name, to which he'd replied earnestly, 'Darling'.

The evening Jerome told his mother he was entering the seminary, she'd gone into the garden and wept.

That was a hot summer too, the summer of his A levels. He thought again of the softly chintzed sitting room, his father rolling back his shirtsleeves, as if facing a problem that could be dealt with, like a blocked drain or a flat tyre. His father, the man Jerome would become, five feet ten, handsomely built with good wide shoulders and a head of dark, somewhat curly hair. He had regarded his only son as the darkness gathered and his wife, dabbing her eyes, came in from the garden to switch on the standard lamp, which she then dimmed, Jerome recalled, as if she couldn't bear to see him too clearly. He'd stood between his liberal humanist parents like a failed saint, unable to work a miracle.

But that was all a long time ago, nearly twenty years, thought Jerome, pushing his trolley through the desiccated sunlight, passing watering cans and bird tables. He had chosen. He had *been* chosen. As his attention returned to his surroundings, he became aware of the red-haired woman again. He paused at some flowers, *Phacelia campanularia*, said the label, and glanced sideways at her; she was wearing a green sundress printed with small white daisies which tied around the neck. She stopped beside him and picked up a tub. 'Busy Lizzies, they're lovely, aren't they?' she said.

'Are they easy to grow?'

'Oh, no trouble, a little water and they're off.'

'That's what I like to hear, I'm not much of an expert at this sort of thing,' said Jerome, adding the flowers to his trolley. A sprinkling of freckles gave the woman a girlish look, but he supposed she must have been around his own age. They stood side by side for a moment, contemplating the busy Lizzies, and next to them, a bunch of springy blue plants.

'They're pretty,' said Jerome, reaching for one.

'Oh, they are, but high maintenance – the supermodels of the plant world.'

'I see,' he said, and laughed.

'I should have rung my mother,' he shrugged, 'she's the gardener in the family. I'm a bit hopeless at all this.'

'It's not as difficult as you might think. Trial and error, that's all.'

'Maybe if you've got green fingers.'

The woman looked at her hands, the backs of which were also lightly sprinkled with freckles. 'Nope,' she said, 'just a bit speckled.'

'I suppose I could fill the whole garden with busy Lizzies.'

'That's one solution.'

'Or maybe I could copy you,' he said, peering into her trolley. 'What are all those in there?'

She named the plants for him one by one; he told her he was impressed.

'It's easy when you're interested,' she said. He nodded and looked back at his lonely busy Lizzies.

'Ah well,' he smiled, about to bid her goodbye.

'Tell you what, I could give you a hand, if you like. I've got everything I need now.'

Jerome had less than an hour before Michael came to collect him, and it would be good to have some guidance, but he hesitated. The woman registered his uncertainty. 'It's no trouble, honestly, I love gardening – almost as much as giving advice.' She smiled and he relaxed.

'Well, if you're sure. That's very kind.'

'Sure. I'm Clare, by the way.'

'Jerome.'

'Like Jerome K. Jerome?'

'Exactly,' he said. Like the writer, for once, rather than the saint after whom he'd taken his name, an ascetic who'd spent a lifetime revising the Bible. As they began to walk she talked about *Three Men in a Boat*, and recounted the incident with the sardine key, which he'd long ago forgotten, though he laughed anyway, buoyed by her good humour. They wheeled their trolleys through the paved walkways, and she pointed out plants of interest, making recommendations as they went.

At some seedlings she paused, 'Oh look, these are the ones my kids are growing at school.'

He nodded. 'How old are your children?'

'Oh, they're not *mine*. I'm a teacher. Little ones.'

He looked down at the baby plants again, imagining her in a room of dusty light surrounded by children.

This was the natural opportunity, this is when he should tell her about himself. *Say something*, he thought, *it isn't difficult. The other priests who share the garden . . . Father McCormack, who did the planting last year . . . I don't have church duties today so I thought I'd take the opportunity*. It was easy. *Easy*. But he remained silent. Instead, he followed her, listening as she explained how dahlias could be planted for a burst of colour in late summer, though it was important not to select the shades too carefully or you lost the element of surprise.

'Every garden needs some chaos,' she said; 'it's like life, you don't want it too well plotted.' They reached an arrangement of hanging baskets.

'How about some of these? Is it a large house?' she asked. Then, as if worried she'd been too curious, 'Only it might affect the choice of basket.'

'Yes, quite large.' He thought of the Victorian parish house he shared with Michael and David, the crumbling red façade that would have been splendid once, the dark mahogany furniture, the garden where he'd sat in the cool of the evening preparing his homily for Pentecost Sunday. He had spoken about the gift of the Holy Spirit, the Spirit that leads people to change their lives, the same Spirit that

94

had visited the disciples in their upstairs room at the first Pentecost, entering as a great wind, settling on their heads like tongues of flame, burning within them, leading them to go into the streets to proclaim the Kingdom of God. Jerome had contemplated his own conversion, how he'd sat in his teenage bedroom, books lying open on the bed, volumes of theology and philosophy, Kant, St Augustine. His parents had appreciated the confusion of adolescence, they'd allowed him to flirt with Catholicism as if he were a young Oscar Wilde musing on the pain and beauty of life, but they had only regarded it as a phase; his religious phase. That night in his room Jerome had been thinking and thinking for hours, but his thoughts dissolved when the great wave of the Spirit descended upon him without warning. He'd been overcome, knocked flat out on the floor, and all his questions had disappeared because he saw his life before him. Like St Paul at Damascus, God had called him. Like the disciples in the upstairs room, he had been chosen, he had felt the fire in his head moving into his heart. He knew then, at seventeen, that he had received his vocation.

But last Sunday, looking out on to his congregation – a clutch of older people, mostly women, a few young families, one or two couples – he had delivered the words of his sermon and felt nothing. He might have been a newscaster reading a report. Afterwards, during the communion still, he'd shut his eyes and tried again to pray, thinking of Psalm 104, '*He who maketh his angels spirits; his ministers a flaming fire.*' Of all times, Pentecost must surely be his time of renewal. But he'd felt nothing.

Clare didn't ask any more questions. 'Three of these baskets should balance the space,' she said, 'and you'll need something to fill them with.'

'What are my options?'

'Fuchsias are nice, or nasturtiums, or . . .' She put her hands out to a bed of white blossoms and stroked a petal with the edge of her thumb. The nail was painted with a light polish. 'You could fill the basket with flower trailers.'

'What do you think?'

She looked around for a moment, considering. Her eyes were green, grey-green, and the brows a little darker than her hair.

'Personally, I like the smaller ones. *Lotus berthelotii* are pretty.'

'What colour are they?'

'Orangey red, like little jewels.'

'Perfect.'

'And how about some *Tolmiea menziesii*? Their name means mother of thousands.'

Like the church, Jerome nearly said.

They walked on in silence for a couple of minutes, looking about them. An elderly woman with a parasol passed and gave them a smile. When Jerome's trolley was nearly full they circled back to the busy Lizzies.

'Right, well, I suppose I just have to hope for the best now,' said Jerome. 'Thank you, you've been very kind.'

'My pleasure,' she said. The sun was still fierce at four thirty and she put a hand up to shield her eyes. 'It was nice meeting you.'

'You too.'

She shifted her shoulder bag. 'Listen, why don't I give you my number,' she said, rummaging for a pen, 'in case you need some advice with the planting?'

Despite himself, Jerome felt pleased as Clare wrote down the number on a scrap of paper and gave it to him. They exchanged a smile, and she held his gaze for a long moment before glancing at her watch. 'Right, I'm all done.' She turned her trolley towards the tills. Jerome half hesitated, as if about to follow, but stood still. 'Goodbye, Jerome K. Jerome,' she called over her shoulder. 'Don't be afraid to ring.'

When she'd disappeared, Jerome unfolded the slip of paper. *Clare Bryce*, it said, the letters round and neat from writing the alphabet over and over again. Then a mobile number.

He waited a few minutes then paid for the plants and found a bench near the car park where he could enjoy the shade and wait for Michael. There was a haze over the cars and their bonnets shimmered in the sunlight, like the shells of brightly coloured insects. In one of the bays nearby, Jerome could see a man in sunglasses waiting behind the steering wheel of his car. Every now and again, the man looked in Jerome's direction. After five minutes or so, Jerome began to wonder if the man recognised him. Perhaps he was a parishioner? He was forever trying to remember names and faces in shops and supermarkets. After a little while the man got out of his car and walked over. He was tall, with a trimmed beard and he walked with a long, easy stride. When he reached Jerome, he took off his sunglasses.

'Good afternoon,' he said, 'I was wondering if I could speak with you?' Jerome nodded. 'I was wondering if I could speak with you about Jesus?'

So he was a parishioner. Jerome struggled, but couldn't place him. Before he could enquire, the man was speaking again.

'Have you accepted Jesus as your saviour?' The man stood in a patch of sunlight and looked seriously at Jerome sitting on the bench, surrounded by the polystyrene tubs of seedlings and the new hanging baskets. For a moment he didn't understand, then he realised, the man was evangelising. Perhaps used to being dismissed, the man followed up his question quickly by reaching into his satchel and taking out a booklet.

'May I offer you this? I feel that Jesus wants you to accept him into your life.' Jerome took the booklet and looked into the face of the man who was saying these things to him. It was a kind face with a glittering of perspiration on the brow. The booklet was called 'Faith in Our Times' and on the cover was a large pencil drawing of a cross.

'I'm Jason,' said the man, 'and this is my church. The address is here.' He pointed to the corner of the page. 'You're very welcome to drop by any time if you'd like to see how we worship, or if you'd just like to talk.'

'Thank you,' said Jerome.

'I know many people feel uncomfortable in churches, but ours is very informal. We're always happy to receive visitors; there are questions everyone asks themselves, at some point or other.' The man continued like this, telling Jerome about the healing power of God, about the fact that God is always calling us to him, even if we do not hear.

Jerome let him speak. When he stopped, Jerome said, 'Tell me, why is it that God suddenly calls some people, and then, just as suddenly, leaves them?'

There was a pause, and the man nodded to him, listening, encouraging.

'Why is it, why is it that he chooses to make himself known and then withdraws again? Surely a loving God shouldn't abandon, shouldn't turn away . . .'

The man said calmly, 'He never turns away from us, we turn away from him.' It was the sort of answer that Jerome himself might have given. The man said, 'Sometimes, it's about waiting for God to speak. Trust. Patience. A matter of faith.'

'But if someone has been faithful, forsaken everything.' Jerome could feel his breathing quicken, his chest tightening with anger.

'So, you have a relationship with God?' asked the man.

'I . . . I . . .' Jerome stopped himself. What was he doing speaking like this to a stranger in a car park?

Jason nodded seriously, as if he understood. 'The literature might help.'

Jerome thanked him. Jason put on his sunglasses again and walked back across the hot tarmac to his car. He got into the driver's seat but didn't move off; instead he continued to sit perfectly still, like someone conducting a stakeout. Jerome felt relieved when Michael pulled up in the old silver Citroën.

Jerome liked Michael. He was a sandy-haired Jesuit in his late fifties who'd spent eighteen years in the missions. His was a practical faith. In his work he'd seen the very worst of human nature – children tortured, women beaten – but he'd remained steadfast. And here he was now in West Norwood, having obeyed his superiors by returning to London, going where he was needed, delivering the Eucharist to an elderly parishioner then collecting Jerome from a garden centre.

Jerome had sometimes thought about discussing his concerns with Michael, but had decided against it. Anyway, how could he explain? Did he doubt the existence of God? His reason as much as his experience convinced him of that existence, but he could not feel God as he once had. He was like a man who had lost all sense of touch, who could see and hear, but could not smell or taste; in his soul, he could no longer feel.

The two men loaded the bags into the car, chatting about nothing in particular. As they drove through the entry gate, back towards the main road, they passed a line of young trees, their leaves turned to yellow medallions in the sun.

'The grandeur of God, eh?' said Michael.

'Hmm?'

'*It will flame out like shining from shook foil*,' quoted Michael. 'Don't tell me you don't know your Gerard Manley Hopkins.'

'Ah, of course. Sorry.' They'd reached a queue of commuter traffic and the car slowed, Michael driving on the clutch. Jerome rolled down the window all the way as the car crawled along, turning over the last line of the poem in his head: *The Holy Ghost over the bent world broods with warm breast and with ah! Bright wings*. He thought of Hopkins living his solitary life, denying himself his longing to write poems. Hopkins the Jesuit. Hopkins the convert.

His fingers moved to his breast pocket where Clare's number lay, hidden like a seed. Perhaps he would ring her and then, on the phone, he could make the nature of his life known to her. Otherwise she might go home to her garden and feel despondent or wondering; she might think he had not liked her, when he had liked her. He had liked her very much.

The booklet was still rolled up in his hand, and now he flicked through it, resting a moment on a passage from Corinthians '. . . *there hath no temptation taken you but such as is common to man: but God is faithful, who will not suffer you to be tempted above that ye are able; but will with the temptation also make a way to escape, that ye may be able to bear it*.'

Jerome wondered why, if the leaflet was reaching out to the person in the street, the editors had chosen the King James translation of the Bible. He rolled it up and slid it into the glove compartment.

'What's that?' asked Michael.

'Oh, something a man gave me outside the garden centre. He must have been evangelical or Pentecostal. He was trying to convert me.'

'Go on!' laughed Michael. 'That's what comes from not wearing the collar,' he said. 'Did he have any luck?'

'Not a chance,' said Jerome, 'I'm a lost cause.' Michael laughed again. Jerome turned back to the window.

Speak to me, he said silently. *Speak to me.*

The car gathered speed and passed a bank of hot orange flowers. Marigolds? Clare would know. Jerome shut his eyes as the car accelerated, feeling the breeze from the open window rushing against his face, the flash of orange flowers massing behind his eyelids. He tilted his head further to feel the heat and wind fall on him and in a hot blur he received an image of Clare, her hair flickering around her shoulders, the beginning of a fire in his head.

LOIS McEWAN

Mrs Laidlaw's Event Horizon

MRS LAIDLAW should have followed Newton's second law, her body accelerating in proportion to the strength of external force used upon it as she flew across the living room, until she hit the opposite wall. There, under Newton's third law, the action of the wall would cause an equal and opposite reaction; Mrs Laidlaw would slide down it in a heap.

But a black hole had opened up in the living room of 23A Morningside Drive. Mrs Laidlaw had reached the point of no return and was about to disappear from the visible universe. As she collapsed to her infinite density, she was simultaneously smeared on the event horizon and would for ever see herself being annihilated behind the yellow sofa.

No knowledge of events inside the event horizon can ever be passed to the outside world, not even to Mrs Laidlaw's sister. Beyond the event horizon is the photon-sphere, where Mrs Laidlaw's memory is trapped, driven by centripetal forces to orbit the black hole for ever. Even if her body was able to reconstitute itself enough to leave the house in one piece, on two feet say, rather than in a box, her mind would never leave that room. It is still in orbit even as we speak and may never come down again.

What exactly was burnt on to Mrs Laidlaw's brain for all eternity is not clear. Sometimes she thought it was all her own fault; but any body, anybody, can become a black hole if they collapse down far enough.

As Mrs Laidlaw followed the extreme curvature of space-time around the couch, one black Manolo Blahnik (size 5) rose from a cleft in the cushions and rejoined her left foot. The tear in her Ghost dress knitted together in a genuine invisible mend as the fabric turned from crimson to white. A spray of blood spots lifted from the yellow upholstery and fitted around her throat like a ruby necklace as she flew back to where Mr Laidlaw stood in the doorway with the blade.

Mr Laidlaw took the knife across her throat and put his fist around it. Mrs Laidlaw's eyes bulged and her face changed from pink to white. Mr Laidlaw walked over to the sink and put the knife down on the draining board. Coffee lifted from Mr Laidlaw's front in a glittering brown arc and poured itself back into Mrs Laidlaw's cup, leaving his shirt snow-white, like a washing powder advert.

A stream of hot air, toothpaste and spittle flew into Mr Laidlaw's mouth as the shrieks of rage beyond speech turned to invective:

hrrgra hrrgra gals gnikcuf, gals uoy, tnuc gnikcuf, hctib hctib

So, will we miss the mortgage payment again this month? asked Mrs Laidlaw.

The law said that for every action, there was an equal and opposite reaction; a tooth for a tooth, an eye for an eye, blood for coffee. But although they resembled each other in colour, consistency and perhaps even quantity, to Mrs Laidlaw it was not an equal reaction, it was an over-reaction. Oh yes.

Newton said that her throat exerted an equal force on Mr Laidlaw's fist, but Mrs Laidlaw had not found it so. Her throat, and other parts of her, underwent changes which Mr Laidlaw did not. Changes in colour, to magenta, midnight blue or perhaps indigo, like a goth's eye-shadow palette, but let's not get into black eyes, let's not go there right now. She also changed shape; parts of Mrs Laidlaw swelled and burst. She became deformed, as if she inhabited some dystopian underworld, which indeed she did, while Mr Laidlaw remained much the same, outwardly at least.

Mr Laidlaw was cleaning his teeth. He put on his jacket while Mrs Laidlaw took a cup of coffee out of the microwave and poured it back into the jug. They put on their coats and went downstairs in stony silence. A cab appeared outside. Mrs Laidlaw paid the driver. Mr Laidlaw looked at her and fumbled sheepishly in his pockets.

They drove to the Regency casino in Royal Circus. It was just opening. Mrs Laidlaw stood clutching her evening bag, knuckles white. Mr Laidlaw sat down at the roulette table. The croupier pushed Mr Laidlaw's last £500 chip, his last tiger, back on to the table. The wheel of fortune spun. *Les jeux ne sont pas faits.* Mr Laidlaw took his tiger off number 13 and rolled it back, orange and black, orange and black, across the table and into his pocket.

The croupier drove a streak of tigers towards Mr Laidlaw. He picked them up and stood, enjoying the tiddlywink noise they made as they ran from hand to hand. Mr Laidlaw's tigers were rare, an endangered species. He took the chips to the cashier's window and changed them into money. Then he went to the cashpoint and put money into the little slot. This experiment was repeated several times, under the silent supervision of Mrs Laidlaw. The results were consistent; chips were transformed into cash, very rarely the other way round. Then they went home.

Mr Laidlaw sat on the bed, took off his shoes and socks.

Mrs Laidlaw ran in, holding his grey and white argyle socks. She had found them in the chest in the spare room. Then she ran downstairs, to rake frantically through the dirty laundry in the basket, pants and tights falling out into the cat's bed, although she knew the socks were not there.

Why can't you just put my socks in my sock drawer? shouted Mr Laidlaw. It's not exactly rocket science.

Mrs Laidlaw had thought she had put them in there, the top-left drawer on his dressing table. She ran downstairs. She looked in the washing machine, although she knew it was empty, and spun the drum in case they had wrapped themselves around it. She ran down the garden, Manolos sticking in the mud, to check they were not fluttering on the washing line. What are you doing, running round outside in your long dress like a madwoman? she thought.

Mrs Laidlaw ran inside. She had lost the plot. She was beginning to think she was losing her mind. She seemed to spend her time running round in circles, going faster and faster but falling further and further behind with bits of her falling off and her hair all everywhere like the White Queen in *Alice in Wonderland* going oh God oh God oh God

She ran upstairs.

So where are they? yelled Mr Laidlaw. He took off his belt and waved it at her.

But I know I put them in there.

They weren't.

They aren't.

Mrs Laidlaw sometimes wondered if Mr Laidlaw secretly hid his socks, and other items, to give him an excuse to punish her and to make her think she was going mad. Things moved around the house in ways not covered by Newtonian laws. A golfing trophy vanished from the sideboard and was found weeks later in the shed. His cuff links migrated to the soap dish. But she was mad to even think he would do that, paranoid.

She did not understand the chemical reactions that took place inside Mr Laidlaw. He was made of some unstable substance liable to spontaneously combust but had not been correctly labelled. X: irritant, avoid contact with eyes and skin. In case of contact with Laidlaw, rinse immediately and seek medical attention. Laidlaw could lie dormant for weeks, often in front of the television, then explode without warning.

The previous February, for instance, Mrs Laidlaw had gone to stay with her sister in Glasgow. She was lonely. There were lengthy phone calls from Mr Laidlaw. He said he had changed. The marks had almost faded from her neck and upper arms. He sent a card. He promised it would never happen again. There was still some bruising to her inner thigh, but she could walk almost normally. He was terribly sorry. She could go out, wearing heavy make-up, after dark, with her hair trained over the left side of her face. He sent flowers.

Christ almighty, said her sister. I wouldn't have known you.

Mrs Laidlaw limped down the drive, wearing a scarf. She took the last train back to Waverley, long after dark, when no one was out but a few late-night drunks. Some of them had been beaten up too, so nobody took much notice.

She took a cab back to 23A Morningside Drive. In the bedroom, Mr Laidlaw had passed out and was snoring. Shards of the dressing-table mirror glittered on the carpet like a shoal of stranded fish. The heel of one of her stilettos was stuck in a jar of face cream. She took her coat off and crept into bed in the spare room without waking him.

Time stopped. Everything was frozen, crystallised water falling white in the darkness, the ice skating over the glass. Her breath formed steaming clouds in the cold air of the bedroom, gas to liquid, water to solid. But her face was liquefying; her flesh was soft and puffy, melting into blood, wine, snot and tears smeared across her hands.

Mrs Laidlaw had another drink. She was not sure she still existed. There was a moaning noise. A monster had got stuck in her mirror, its nose everywhere and the eyes gone.

Mrs Laidlaw had a drink. She couldn't think how it had started. She lay down on the floor. Everything was quiet. She was still alive because bits of her hurt. She could hear him smashing something in the bedroom. He stopped and went away. She hoped she would not die. She closed her eyes and waited for it to stop. She was lying on the floor, her face in the burnt smell of the carpet, things coming at her too fast to see, faster than the speed of sound.

She asked Mr Laidlaw to stop inserting his penis in Mrs MacAllister. Mr Laidlaw explained that Mrs MacAllister was made of such a dense substance that her gravity exerted an unnatural force on his trousers, making them fall to the floor whenever he was in her vicinity. He would have kept his distance, but Mrs MacAllister's magnetic field attracted his opposite pole.

Well, yes.

You are seeing someone, aren't you? said Mrs Laidlaw. Is it Mrs MacAllister?

You're paranoid. There's no one else.

You've been with someone else, said Mrs Laidlaw.

Mr Laidlaw went out for a few days.

Mrs Laidlaw lay in bed, drinking gin and eating frozen yoghurt. Time slowed down. The agency gave up waiting for her to come back to work and hired someone else. She watched TV or sometimes the wall. Flowers swarmed over the white plaster, translucent daisies with petals bursting open into silver stars, their spiralling fractels climbing up the curtains to the ceiling. Mrs Laidlaw put on her dressing gown.

Mr Laidlaw came back.

No, you're too ugly, he said.

Mrs Laidlaw lay naked on the bed. Mr Laidlaw was on his mobile in the garden. Maybe it was a work call. Mr Laidlaw got in from work at 10 p.m. Mrs Laidlaw had a bath and painted her toenails. Mr Laidlaw was working late again.

Under Newton's law of inertia, Mrs Laidlaw found her internal resistance to getting out of the house or her dressing gown increased. Although she was no longer carrying the baby, she was heavier instead of lighter, as if it was still there but made of lead. She went to the Royal Infirmary and stayed in overnight. She miscarried. Mr Laidlaw drove her home.

You're not that bad, are you?

ahhhh

You must have done it to yourself.

ahhhhh

You fell over my foot.

ahhhh

Had you been at the wine?

ahhhh

You never look where you're going.

ahhhh

Stop making that noise

ahhhh

Better ring your sister. You won't be able to go now, will you?

ahhhh

The bleeding wouldn't stop. Mrs Laidlaw lay at the bottom of the stairs. She did a somersault up the staircase to where Mr Laidlaw stood on the landing. He took hold of her and they struggled, locked together like dancers. Her teeth rattled in her head like castanets.

You're so fucking selfish, he said.

You'll all be too blethered to notice who's there and I can't drink anything, she said.

It'll look bad. All the other wives will be there.

But you told me it was next week.

You said you'd come to the club dinner.

I'll just go to my sister's on my own then.

I'm not driving over to Glasgow just to go to a fucking party. Your sister hates me. She always has. Gone native and turned into a bloody weegie.

It's her big night.

She didn't even come to our wedding.

The wedding had been a surprise, as if held on a sudden romantic impulse. Everyone except Mrs Laidlaw, who became Miss Ruthven, drank a lot. Miss Ruthven was pregnant.

She woke up under Mr Laidlaw. She was confused. Time speeded up and slowed down. She was sick. Miss Ruthven spent a lot of time in darkened rooms with flashing lights as part of a mass experiment into the effects of methylenedioxmethamphetamine on the human brain. This stimulated the secretion of, and inhibited the re-uptake of, serotonin, dopamine and norepinephrine. As well as euphoria, synaesthesia and entheogenia, these chemicals had unfortunate side effects such as bruxism (teeth-grinding), trisma (jaw-clenching), nystagmus (shutter vision) and finding someone like Laidlaw attractive, particularly in places where conversation was impossible due to industrial levels of noise.

Miss Ruthven went to university. She left her friends' flat in Thistle Street and moved in with her parents at 6 Canaan Lane. Space was constrained in the Ruthven household.

You've ruined my life, said Miss Ruthven.

You've ruined dinner, said Mr Ruthven. Your mother has gone to a lot of trouble to make nice food. You're very selfish.

Knives spun in circles, the saltcellar jigged on the spot. Mr Ruthven's fork clattered off the floor and flew up on to the table. Mr Ruthven banged his fist on the table, which resonated like a gorilla's chest.

If you ever THUMP do that to me again THUMP I'll stop you going to university THUMP. If I say infinite means small THUMP then in this house THUMP it means small THUMP.

But Dad, infinite means endless, like, very big. The universe is infinite. You mean infinitesimal.

It was infinite, said Mr Ruthven, holding up his finger and oppositional thumb a millimetre apart. There was infinite space between his bumper and mine. And he said he hadn't boxed me in.

Mr Ruthven stopped the car. Miss Ruthven got out. She ran along the verge after the car. Mr Ruthven stopped, waited until she reached the car then drove off. She ran along the verge after the car. Mr Ruthven stopped, waited until she reached the car then drove off. She ran along the verge after the car going oh no oh no oh no

Mr Ruthven drove off. Miss Ruthven tried to open the door. She went over to the trees and was sick all over her shoes. She ran back to the car and jumped in.

Now all those cars will overtake us and I'll have to overtake them again. There goes that Jag already.

Mr Ruthven stopped.

Not again.

BLURRRGGHHHH

You won't. Just look out of the window.

I'm going to be sick.

Mr Ruthven had accelerated, increasing his momentum until he broke the sound barrier and was unable to hear anything.

Dad, I feel sick.

He was an unstoppable force. He was breaking the law, nee naw nee naw. Laws did not apply to him.

Dad, I feel sick.

The speed of his reactions meant he could drive at 135mph, corner at 110.

Look, I can steer with my knees, said Mr Ruthven, waving his hands in the air as they barrelled along, overtaking a white van, a couple of Fords and a Jaguar.

People are terrified by the speed of my brain, said Mr Ruthven. My reactions are so fast. That's why I always win at squash.

He was quite alarming. He never lost, not even at tiddlywinks or snap. He honed his reactions by throwing Miss Ruthven up and down over the stairwell, shouting with glee as her eyes widened with terror every time he let her go. Her attention was focused on him, nothing but him, he had the power of life and death. He was infallible, invincible.

He blotted her out. Miss Ruthven remembered nothing. She knew it was too much, even then, too much, but it was already too late. Mr Ruthven caught her and everything went black. Then he ran back across the living room away from her. He tripped over the stool, which made him even more angry.

Miss Ruthven dodged round the stool. It was below Mr Ruthven's line of vision so she knew he would trip over it, which would give her more time, but she knew he would get her in the end.

I told you not to do that, he yelled. I told you. Put your clothes back on.

Mr Ruthven appeared in the doorway, a giant blocking out the light. She ran out into the garden, her clothes trailing across the grass. The daisies were white stars in a green sky, the dandelions burning suns. She was a naked singularity who could not be allowed to exist going faster and faster and faster until she disappeared . . .

MÁIRE COONEY

Is This What You Want?

THAT YOURS?

    Two words. Just that. A simple question. But you've hesitated. You'd better say something. Say anything. Say

  Hmmm?

  That's fine. You've bought a few seconds.

  This. Found it on the floor, under the seat. Wee cross and chain thing.

  Which of course you know very well, have seen close up. But fine, OK. Take it easy now. Eyes on the road. It could be yours, why not? You could take a look.

  Might be, I can't see it. Hold it over.

  Good. Another few seconds. Look across and

  Mind the road! Jesus.

  Better. A slight swerve as you glance over. Brilliant actually.

  Don't think it's mine. One of the kids?

  Oh, maybe.

  Your Mum's?

  Hardly.

  You did OK there. You're feeling pleased with yourself. And why not? Despite the clear hesitation, the slight quickening of the heart, you got through it. It'll come up again most likely, he's still holding it, twirling it in his fingers for God's sake, but you've got it covered. You're quite good at this, better than you thought. Really. Turn it around; you'd have got the whole story before you were back at the house. He'd have broken down, confessed the whole thing. No he wouldn't. He wouldn't have fucked a casual acquaintance in the first place. Someone on hellohowareyou terms before a sudden, blinding, mutual realisation of what you wanted to do to each other. As if. But this is an amusing thought, you go with it, picture the scene.

What's so funny?

He often interrupts at the wrong time.

Just thinking about something. Work stuff. Nothing.

What, he says. Tell me.

Really. You wouldn't find it funny.

Which is true.

It was unexpected, as good sex often is, and the way you threw yourself into it suggests it's something you might get a taste for. As it were. You like the slight split inside your top lip, like running your tongue over it, remembering. You like the broken skin on your back too. Before this, your last carpet burns were followed by detention, a stern talking to. Young ladies did not fight. But you're not so young now. And this, you feel certain, is much more ladylike. This is good. All in all, a good thing. But not uncomplicated.

They spring at the car as you pull up, hang on the doors, the small one bouncing, mouth wide, hands flat on the glass, the bigger one watching you, opening your door. This could be endearing, flattering even. Except

JIGET IT?

this from the bigger one, and

CAPUTERCAPUTER CAPUT UUR

from the smaller. You did get it, PC World. Not a bad deal, all in all. Not a bad distraction either. This brainwave,

116

following your second, quite astonishing, quite breathtaking, meeting – fling just doesn't do it – with the casual acquaintance. About time we got one, you'd said, the kids are getting older. Something for all of us.

You, of course, have something all for yourself. For once. Twice. Twice isn't an affair. Twice is worse than once, certainly, but it could stop there. A nohardfeelings whatwerewethinking end to it. It could end, it could just stop. Dead. You've thought that, more than once. And, more than once, have felt cold at the thought. Actually cold. Crushed ice in your veins. Numb weight in your lungs.

The next time is planned. Nothing said, but planned all the same. A Wednesday, early afternoon. You answer the door, lead him through. You can't think of anything to say. You forget if you've exchanged words before. You must have. And you stare, smile. You nod. You should speak.

Hi.

Which is a start. And

You OK?

Rhetorically, really, because you're so close you can feel his breath on your lips, asking you to sit, just sit, fingertips brushing your forearm, the lightest touch, hardly touching at all, tracing your shoulder, the hollow of your neck, eyes fixed on you, locked, then both hands behind your neck, holding you, because now you're falling, teeth touching, then lips, widening, and you're breathing for each other, mouths tugging, holding, then pulling, tearing, at buttons, zips, hands reaching round, skin and salt, tasting, touching, pushing, closer, into him, into you, listening to him, or you, you can't tell which, you honestly can't tell, struggling; all noise and burning impatience, to get further.

Further is not where you should be going with this. This

thought as you sit, after, coffee in one hand, tapping the rim to disguise the shaking, drown out the blood thumping in your ears, loud in the room. You're watching him speak, watching the mouth opening, closing. You don't hear the words. You watch the face; a beautiful, pale, open face, and the eyes; a lighter blue than you can name; the oldest denim, a memory of blue. You wipe one hand on your lap, holding the mug with the other, then swap hands, readjust your grip. He's still talking. Bits come through, fragments. Orkney. Wind rain sheep, all true. Edinburgh was England, ha ha.

Ha ha, you say. Maybe a little loudly. But he smiles, continues. Is this what people do? You have no idea. People who have affairs? Drink coffee after, exchange life stories. Then what? That's the thing. What then? And now you're frowning, must be because he's asking about spouses, children, the time; laughing, saying something about under the bed, out the window. Ha ha. You should say something now. There's a silence and it's because you have to say something. You say

It's fine. Really, go on. You were saying.

Like that. Like it was a coffee morning. And so you listen, hear. Glasgow. Bedsits. Parties. You hear: missed seminars and two ones, thinking about teaching, maybe, maybe when older. Jesus, how old is he? And you've said that out loud because now he's saying, how old do you think? Smiling, enjoying the question. How old do you think? You think, not very, not old at all. Young. You say

I don't know. Twenty-eight? Thirty?

Which is very funny. Hysterical. Do I look that old, he's saying, really? And no, actually, he does not. But that's quite a bit younger than you are and my God, he does not look old at all. Another silence. And then

118

I'd better get going. I'll call you, will I? I'll text you.

A truly modern affair. It has to end; you knew that from the beginning. Not now though, not yet. You like a challenge, you always did. And right now you want it all.

The problem with that, Rob's saying, is the timing. Childcare, you know, all that. It's not easy to sort out, is it? I mean it isn't, is it, just like that? Rob likes to make a point in several different ways. But he's trying to be reasonable and, bless him, is trying not to show impatience; Rob doesn't show anger, with the suggestion. He's cutting chillies, head low over the chopping board; cutting fast, hard, knife pounding them into the board. So you try again, gently, stroke his arm as you talk.

I'll be gone three nights, Rob.

He's listening but not warming to it and you'd better make this good and so

I wasn't so much asked as told.

Not really true. And

If I could get out of it, believe me

Believe me I would not.

The chillies are all but pulped, a red mash. He lifts one hand to his eye, rubs it and

Fuck. Ow!

And bends his head, rubs his eye again.

Ow! Jesus.

You take him by the hands, lead him to the sink, scoop cold water over his angry reddened eyes. It occurs to you right then that you're enjoying life, really enjoying it. You like looking after Rob, the kids, the home. You're good at it. You like your job, you're good at that too. And you like, you really like, the extras; snatched, grabbed at, whenever, wherever, circled on the kitchen calendar as

119

dentist appointment, book club, work drinks and, perhaps, conferences. Best of all you enjoy the way you manage it all, beautifully. Back to the conference though, your idea, and nearly won. He's still dabbing his eyes.

You OK?

It really hurt, he says.

I know, baby. Look, the conference. It doesn't matter, I'll tell them I can't, the children

No.

And he's insisting now, his idea.

You go. We'll be fine. Really.

Really?

I want you to go.

You could have scripted it.

You drive back separately. No sense in pushing your luck. The drive back is wonderful: quiet roads, a clear night. You're a better mother for this, a better spouse, you really are. Quality not quantity, that's the thing. You need to keep on your toes, sure, juggle things. Nobody said it was easy. And you could do with more time, just a little more time. You could take it from work maybe, you have an exemplary work record. A four-day week, they'd go for that, three's maybe pushing it, but who knows. Keep your options open, you can deal with it later. You can deal with anything.

Rob's still up when you get in, sitting in front of the box. Not like him at all. Easy though, take it easy, talk to him.

Hi darling. You're up late. Your eyes dancing, checking the room. He's not drinking, good, could be anything. How're the kids?

Fine. How was the conference?

The way he says it is wrong. Too light, too quick. You

turn to him, check your instinct. You're right of course. He's pulling at his lip, frowning.

Oh God.

The best you can manage.

You might have covered yourself at the office, he says. Sheila phoned.

Take your time. Let him tell you what he knows.

So where were you? he says. Where were you the past four days?

He doesn't know. He doesn't know any of it. You smile, you can't not, turn it into a nervous laugh. This isn't over.

I had to get away.

Why?

A reasonable question. Throws you.

Why did you? His voice quiet now, unsure. Which means he's scared, worried about you. Think. Think. You've never done this before, it's not like you. You're not yourself.

I'm sorry, I'm not myself. I don't know what I was thinking. You snatch a look, and he's watching you, fingers twisting. I get so tired, Rob. And you put your hands to your face, lean into them, as a tired person might do. You wait, wait, and yes, a hand on your neck, pulling you nearer. You lean into him, exhausted, ecstatic.

It doesn't last. It never does. You may well have made things worse. But don't beat yourself up, you had to think on your feet. You walked into an awkward situation and dealt with it. You've got yourself a new problem now, that's all. Play the jaded, exhausted card and you're asking to be looked after. Closely. And he is watching, he's worried. It's making you nervous. You're not sleeping, you're so hyped. Today. Today you'll find an unwatched hour, half an hour. You can find that much time

Tea?

that much space

Do you want another? That'll be cold.

maybe before you pick up the kids. But he's talking again. You should answer.

What's that?

Tea. D'you want one. I'm making some.

Tea.

Tea. Yes. Thank you.

A reasonable answer, but not the right one. He's still watching you. You can feel it, the way you'd feel someone lean their entire weight on you. Too much. This is too much. Relax. Hum something, fiddle with your nails, he'll go away. He'll go away and then you can text, sort a time.

I don't think you should go in today.

You should text now. You need to plan things, organise them. But he's still talking. You look up, meet his eyes. He's trying to say something and clearly isn't going to stop until you give whatever the right answer is. The question, though. What did he say?

What did you say?

Work. I don't think you should go in. I can phone in for you. I think I should.

Work. God, yes.

No. No, don't be silly, of course I'm going in. I might be late back actually.

It's all about planning, organising. You're a little tired, that's all. Now think

You've not touched that.

think. If he runs the kids in, there's some time right there. You can tell them one of the kids is poorly. Who argues with that? Thank God for kids. A virus, doctor's visit, perfect. You'll phone work on the way, get in mid-morning. OK.

YOURS 930 TEXT IF OK. Send message and, message sent. Good. But he's still there, working himself up to say something.

We need to talk.

Working himself up to a cliché.

When you're finished with your phone. Boys, go and do your teeth.

Properly, you shout after them, give Rob a little smile. You are a good mother. But he's not smiling back and something is most definitely up.

What's going on? he says.

The question feels huge. But he doesn't mean it to be, so you frown, say

How d'you mean?

Pretty feeble, but you're not feeling too great right now, really not too great at all.

You're not eating. You're not sleeping. You look like shit.

He can be direct. And now you're both looking at the table, at your phone which has just buzzed, shifted slightly across the table. You need to pick it up. You need to ignore it. You need it to say *YES 930*. You need to lie down.

Do you want to get that?

What, that? No. No, go on. You were saying.

And slowly, slowly, this is becoming not OK, not OK at all. You see his knuckles whiten as he grips the side of the table and then a voice, the smallest voice, a child's

Mummy

then the face round the door. Your youngest. Eyes like they've never blinked. Arms straight in front of him and hands cupping pink foam. He's saying something about broke and bleeded. You don't remember what to do with this. You have to tell him no

Not now

123

And you're reeling. Watched. Eyes on you. The kids, Rob's, all of them. You can't do this. You need to tell them you can't do it

Now's not a good time, honey

You manage that much but he won't go and you're still here and it won't stop. You want to look away, cover your eyes, curl up small, small. But he's holding something and there's blood, it looks like blood, round his mouth and chin. His hands are full of pink foam and there's another voice now; shrill, scared

Stop please stop

Your voice. Yours. And they're looking at you. You're supposed to do something and you can't remember what and you hear

Please

and

Mummy

and

Is this it then? Is this what you want?

And the next thing is your mouth opening, and a sigh, and then stutters of breath, higher and lighter than your laugh but yours all the same, your mouth wide now and noise pouring. You want to speak, you want to say something but you have no words, nothing.

MARIAN GARVEY

All That's Left

IT IS the weight that attracts her. The bath, which is part
of what has caught her eye, is blue plastic, scuffed white
in places though this doesn't concern Agnes. It is not the
container she's interested in. The cement is wet. A working
sludge. Not still. Though the builders have stopped a while
ago, it has the trace of movement in it. Its surface is firm,
and softly heavy. It's as if someone has recently made the
figure of eight in it with a shovel.

Agnes looks around. Except for Lucy, she is alone in the
courtyard. From where they're sitting on the bench beneath
the honeysuckle, she can see the scaffolding that frames the
brick wall. The rest of the courtyard is lush. Dense green
shrubs try hard to hold back the heat. The French doors are
open. A radio is on somewhere in the house. She doesn't
know where her mother is. Most likely upstairs, lying
down, and the builders have gone, probably to their tea.

Agnes stands up, begins to remove her clothes. 'Hold
these!' Dumps the bundle of dress and knickers and socks
into her sister's arms. Her sister, not realising she's meant to
hold them, drops them. Agnes picks them off the floor. 'Like
this!' She pulls the girl's arms out so they form an awkward
semicircle, which Agnes begins to feed with the clothes.
'Don't drop them! They'll get dirty and Mum'll go mad.'

The girl nods. 'But Agnes!'

'Lucy! Just hold them, will you!'

Agnes takes a step closer to the bath. Her skin is white except for the u shape of sunburn on her back from playing with Lucy, in the sharp heat of the morning.

Just an hour ago, playing in the paddling pool and her mother shouting up to where they were on the top lawn, skidding on the blue sheet of plastic that the hose pipe was running water over, screeching and laughing, both girls stopping the game, whilst Agnes is told she's too old 'for all that jumping about'. Agnes standing in the little blue pool, just waiting till her mother shrugs and gives up and goes back into the house. She has more in common with her mother than her mother realises. Doesn't she know that Lucy is just a baby whereas she is grown up, nearly twelve? Doesn't her mother know anything, like how, it's not the greatest idea to play in a stupid paddling pool but that's all there is, now that everyone's gone and the house is all quiet. Everyone gone back to Ireland. Mum back to work, and she and Lucy back to school for the last week even though the holidays were coming up. 'It'll take your mind off things.' And now, left to play again whilst her mother is upstairs, packing for the six-week jaunt to Ireland, fretting about maps and the motorway, the roof rack, and ferry times.

They'd spent the whole morning playing that game, until Agnes had suggested ducking their heads under the water and it had been funny till Lucy, spluttering and squealing, began to cry, 'Agnes, I can't breathe! Agnes! My eye, my eye . . . I need a towel . . . a towel . . .' and Agnes had told her to 'Shut up, you're fine!' but had still run through the cool of the kitchen, up the stairs two at a time to fetch a towel. It was then she'd heard the noise, a coughing, and instead of the bathroom she'd run down the long corridor to her parents' room, about to push the door wide but stopped in her tracks at the sight of her mother. She'd stood where she was, her swimsuit dripping, watching through the gap in the door. Her mother collapsed against the big bed clutching something. Held against her chest, her mouth open. Agnes could see her teeth and the inside of her mouth. Her mother was shoving something in, filling up the o shape. Her eyes had no tears but her head, her head was staggered back so far Agnes had thought it might fall off. No sound, just the rhythm of her mother's body rocking to and fro, biting into the material. The thing she was holding, one of Daddy's suits. Still on the wooden hanger. The light brown weave of it in her fingers. The trousers stretched out across her lap like she was nursing a child.

She is in now. The sludge of cement at her ankles, skin naked in the afternoon air. Agnes lifting one foot then the other. Paddling. Both girls watching as the creeping sludge drips.

'Stand back, I'm going to lie down.'

'No,' Lucy gasps, but Agnes is already beginning to crouch down.

'Stand back,' says Agnes 'or I'll splash you.'

'But Agnes!' Lucy has the clothes in her arms, is turning first to the right and then, in a panic, to the left, her feet rooted to the spot, she's so afraid she'll drop the clothes. She moves only her upper body, searching for someone, the builders to come back or even their mother. She drops the pants, stares stricken at them lying on the ground.

'Agnes,' she cries, 'I've dropped something!'

But Agnes is already prone. Fits the bath nicely. She begins to lower her head into the cement, the brown liquid crawling round her face and into her earlobes, over her chin, beneath her bottom lip, her hair weaving to the sludge that is framing her face.

Agnes shifts her body a little, feeling the liquid in her ears muting all other sounds. She forgets for a moment where she is. She cannot smell the honeysuckle that is in bloom. What she can smell is the sharpness of dust and stone and wet breathing dirt. She lies back and lets the weight slip over her, a crawling rock on her chest.

'Agnes!' Her sister, crying now.

'What?'

'Mummy . . . will . . .'

'Get some flowers. Over there.' Agnes lifts her arm, raises her body up, and points to one of the flowerbeds. Cement flies everywhere, skiting Lucy with brown droplets. Lucy lets out a scream. It is such a shock. Agnes has been so submerged.

'Pick three or four!'

'Mummy will be cross.'

'Lucy!'

So the young girl does as she is told. She grabs handfuls, quickly ravaging the flowerbeds.

'Come here and stick them in.'

Lucy doesn't move.

'Bring them here!' Agnes is shouting, and Lucy hurries over to the bath, her arms full of sweet peas and alliums. She kneels down and places one of the stems in the cement above Agnes's body. The flower stays upright and Lucy adds another and another.

At first Agnes laughs and tells her it tickles and this makes Lucy smile. With every flower she adds, she looks at Agnes's face, wanting more encouragement, more bossy instructions, but Agnes has gone quiet. So Lucy continues in silence. When she has finished she stands back. She has cement on her hands, which she wipes clean on her dress, and then, absentmindedly, on the bundle of clothes dropped earlier on the ground.

'Agnes,' she whispers, but there is no reply. The girl moves back, under the honeysuckle. Agnes opens an eye, can see the cream brickwork at the back of the kitchen, the steel girders that the builders are using. She listens to sounds muffled by the liquid in her ears. A window opening upstairs, the sash cord rattling, her mother coughing, blowing her nose. She hears Lucy call again but doesn't reply.

In the bath, the cold feels warm. It makes her think of that day; home from school, going into the house, everything still normal, because her mother hadn't spoken yet. Agnes remembers her mother's friend Teresa was there with her hand in the small of her back. As if it was needed. When Agnes had looked to her left, she had seen Lucy watching her from the top of the stairs.

The gentle breath from the cement makes Lucy whisper, 'Agnes!' Then more insistent this time, 'Agnes!'

Exasperated, Agnes lifts up her head, her two hands on the side of the bath, slipping as she tries to keep her grip. Streaks of cement cling to her long hair.

'Lucy! What are you doing?'

'We've got to put the flowers back. Mummy will get cross.'

'Lucy!'

But Lucy is already scooping her arms full of the flowers, the cement streaking her legs, running over to the flower-beds, beginning to shove the flowers back, soil clumping to her fingers, all the while turning back to the bath. 'Agnes, please help! Please help me.'

There is no sound.

So Lucy kneels once more beside the bath, plunges her arms down into the thickness, feels for her sister's hands, rocking the bath with such force the cement starts to slop over the sides. She finds what she's looking for, her own hands slipping trying to get a grip, all the time pulling and pulling till Agnes slowly begins to emerge from the grey.

Lucy murmurs, croons almost as she guides Agnes as if she were blind, helping her to stand, to lift her leg over the side of the bath.

MIRIAM MOSS

Looking In

H<small>E COMES</small> into the room, small and round, with an air of confidence edged with uncertainty. His shock of sandy hair tones with his soft, pink complexion. She is aware of the hard mound of his beer belly resting under his shirt, and thinks how a low centre of gravity must be vital for climbing the long ladders piled on top of his yellow van. He looks intently at her through bloodshot pale blue eyes, his throat folds trembling slightly as he talks.

'To be honest,' he says, 'people don't understand house painting. They say after three weeks: but you said it would only take two, so I have to explain to them about the weather. Surely they've noticed that it rained for three days that week, but no, they just don't remember, do they? I always go out of my way to explain though. After all, you can't paint on wet surfaces, can you?'

'No, I expect not,' she replies. 'I'll be working from home while you're here, so I'll leave coffee and tea out in the kitchen for you to make your own – if you don't mind.'

'Right.' His eyes shift. 'You see, I'm not one to cut corners in my work – but you'll soon realise that. Some painters do, you know.' He expands, talking up his achievements, his way of doing things, how strangers have noticed and praised his work, how ably and quickly he gets things done. How lucky she is that he's prepared to go up high ladders.

'Most young men these days won't think of doing it,' he says, 'and before you know it you've got a bill for a couple of thousand for scaffolding.' She thanks him. He looks satisfied, pleased with her – and then he carries on. She is mesmerised by the weight of his detail, then becomes restless. Her mind wanders, drifting off into what to have for supper. Then she notices his feet. They're in a ballet position, his hips thrust forward.

He goes when he's ready to go. When he's said all he needs to.

When she's been quietened.

The next morning he arrives early, and only when she hears the clanking of ladders does she remember to keep the curtains closed to dress, and feels foolish. He comes into the kitchen to make himself a coffee while she's breakfasting.

'I didn't come in and start until I saw you moving about,' he says, 'I've learnt to be very sensitive about when and where to start, and I'll soon learn your routine.'

But over the next few days he catches her hiding behind the kitchen door in her pyjamas, dashing half naked from the bathroom along the landing. Suddenly he's always there, looking in on her life.

'Having a long weekend are we?' he asks on Monday morning.

'Sorry?'

'Well, you were very slow getting going this morning.' His eyes twinkle.

'I like to arrive early,' he comments over her breakfast. 'But I didn't start painting the bathroom window, I carried on downstairs. So I'll go up there after you've finished, you know, in there.' She feels the shock of him imagining her *in there*. Later she tries to pee silently, wondering if he's outside painting the soil pipe, listening for the flush to run down.

She veers away from him, immersing herself in work. But he comes upstairs to find her, to tell her what he's working on each day, and when he's finished, he comes to tell her what he's done. He starts standing in the doorway of her office, leaning on the chest of drawers as though propping up the bar, holding a pint of beer.

'Families are funny things,' he says. 'I'm an only child and lived with my parents in the same house I was born into – until they died. In the end I sold it. I live alone now.' He pauses. 'Just like you.'

She gets up to make herself a cup of tea.

That night she dreams he's following her around the house, staring at her. She tries to escape him and opens a door into a blank room. But he's already in there. She runs past him and through into another room, and another room. But he's in there every time. She tries shouting for help, but her voice has gone. She mouths and strains, stomach clenched to make herself heard and wakes to the sound of her own groaning.

She starts to dread the sound of his ladders and the sliding of the van's side door. She feels he knows everything about her; that she has Marmite for breakfast, when she starts work, what she has for lunch. He comments on her washing hanging on the line, what's inside her fridge, the pieces of her furniture he particularly likes. He even checks through her post when he picks it up and puts it on the table. She's seen him. She thinks she's becoming paranoid and phones her son, but she doesn't mention it as he's just split up from his girlfriend again, and is morose and monosyllabic.

He starts coming upstairs more and more during the

day, avoiding the creaky stair, as she never hears it. Suddenly he's peering in on her. Once she had her feet up on the desk.

'Oh good, you're not busy,' he says, pushing open the door.

'I was actually,' she says. 'But I've injured my knee.'

And she immediately regrets saying it. Her injured knee was her secret. But he's not interested.

'Just thought you'd like to know I'm off for lunch,' he says.

The next day is very hot and knowing that he's painting round the front, she opens the French windows on the landing. She finishes her call into the office and the phone rings again. It's a long call from a colleague full of jokes and laughter. As soon as she hangs up there's a tap on the open door of her office.

'Ah, you're off the phone,' he says. 'I came earlier but saw you were talking, and then the phone went again so I just sat here on the steps in the sunshine and waited.'

When he goes, she slams the office door and calls a friend.

'He's driving me mad', she says. 'He was sitting there all that time listening.'

'I know what it's like,' her friend says. 'It drove me insane.'

Later he comes in to say which windows she will need to leave open to let the paint harden off overnight.

'It's a good thing I like heights,' he says, 'hauling ladders up on to that roof all day.'

'Yes, I saw you,' she says. He had been sitting straddled across the roof, looking like he owned it. She'd watched him stand up and pirouette away along the apex.

'But I should tell you about my parachute jump,' he says.

'Perhaps another time,' she says quickly. 'You see when I'm in the middle of writing it's hard being interrupted because you have to immerse yourself in the subject all over again.'

'I know what you mean,' he says. 'When I used to do pottery I needed complete concentration. I couldn't bear interruptions. But of course I always got them. That was frustrating I can tell you.'

'Writing can be quite frustrating,' she starts to say.

'I'm sure it is,' he says, 'but I'd better get on. I'll be back to let you know what else I've done before I leave this afternoon.'

'But we've just run through what you're doing today,' she says. 'So we won't need to go through it again, really, will we?'

'I see what you mean,' he says. He looks hard at her for a second and then turns to go.

The next night it rains heavily and he doesn't come. She's ecstatic – but also on edge. Whenever she hears a van door slam her heart sinks. She said that she'd leave the side gate open for him each morning, and now she doesn't know when or if he'll come, when or if she'll find him creeping up to her room.

'Sorry I didn't come yesterday,' he says.

'Oh, it was fine,' she replies. 'As you know, I'm used to absolute privacy, so it was rather nice for a change.'

The next day he doesn't come up to run through everything; how many layers of paint, how deep the scrapings, the ladder angle, how to tie back the plants, how to secure one ladder to another.

But the amnesty only lasts a couple of days.

The office door opens. She feels a hand brush her shoulder and he bangs a pot of paint down on her desk.

'We can't do that bracket black, you know. What about this?' He takes the lid off the paint pot.

'If you think it will tone in,' she says.

'I think it'll do the trick.'

'I'm sure you know best.' She turns back to her computer. He spots a traffic warden through the window.

'You know, they get six quid for every person they nab. I've seen them rocking cars to and fro so that the ticket slides out of sight. I deliberately leave my old tickets all over the windscreen so that it takes them ages to find the right one. They can't get me because I glue them down and then photograph them for proof with my digital camera. I like taking pictures. Though they did try once. I marched into the parking office with my photo and told them where they could put their fine. They didn't have a leg to stand on. But, would you believe it, while I was in there, they were slamming another on my van parked outside. I went back to the girl and I said, "Look, I'm a reasonable man but this is nasty and I know how to be nasty too, and you won't want to see it. So I suggest that you treat me right." She did. I got clear of both. Just need to be firm, you see. I had to tick off the doctor too. She was very rude. Didn't even look up as I went in, and then she had the gall to sigh when I told her about two or three other things that were bothering me, including the boil on my neck. "You need to make a longer appointment if you have a lot of things to discuss," she said. I carried on of course, and at the end I said, "I don't like people who are rude to me, and I don't like your tone. If you speak pleasantly to me I'll be pleasant back, but if you don't you won't like what you'll get at all." She soon showed me some respect. You see I'm like you, with your Marmite for

136

breakfast. I'm very particular. Don't eat any vegetables or fruit. Hate them. That woman tried to tell me that was why I had this recurring boil. Talk about ignorant! It got as big as a cricket ball. She had to lance it. It was full of pus, you see. But she's absolutely hopeless because it's coming back again.' He points. 'I can feel it. I'll have to go and tell her – so I'll be going early today.'

It was raining heavily when she woke the next morning. He won't come, she thought. He won't come in this. She is so elated she turns up the radio and dances round the kitchen. She spins and twirls – and sees a figure going past the window.

'Hello,' he says, putting his head round the door. 'You're having fun.'

She snaps the radio off.

'Why have you come? It's pouring.'

'Oh, I've been sitting outside to see if it will let up. I parked just below the garden and I've been sitting in the van for an hour and a half or so, reading the paper and getting out now and then to see if you've come down.'

She feels drained and shrunken.

'But I've been down for ages. And it isn't letting up at all,' she says.

'No. But I saw that you were up, and then I waited until I could see you moving about downstairs before I came in to say I think I won't be coming in. But if it dries up a bit this afternoon, I might.'

'If it's pouring with rain all night and still is when you wake up,' she says, 'I don't see why you come here at all. Why don't you just stay at home and ring me to let me know when you'll be in?'

But she knows why.

She goes to her room, closes all the blinds and locks herself in.

For the last few days he imports a gnarled drinking companion to help him. He has close, shifty eyes, a grey complexion and a loud phlegmy cough. She tries to eat breakfast while he crouches on the back step smoking and painting the doorframe, and gobbing up phlegm the size of small jellyfish on to the garden path.

The two men take long lunch breaks in the sunshine on the decking opposite her closed office door. Eventually she forces herself outside to take in the washing.

'When do you think you might be finished?' she asks.

'Maybe next week or the week after,' he says. 'All depends on the weather.'

It rains all weekend and is sunny on Monday.

Please hurry up, she screams inwardly. But he's out on the pavement chatting to the people in the street. He knows all her neighbours now. He comes in to make a cup of coffee while she's cleaning the kitchen.

'Just got another job.'

'Did you.'

'People from Number Sixteen want their front doing, and the people at Number Twenty asked me to do their railings.'

'You'll be painting the whole street soon,' she says.

'Yes, and it's not surprising, I suppose,' he says. 'My work is its own advertisement. To be honest, they can see if a job's well done. That's why I'm being asked by everyone round here.'

At last there's only a little bit of railing to do at the front and a pipe at the back. He phones her that evening.

'Looks like it might rain tomorrow, so I was thinking that perhaps I'd come by first thing and then you can give me the side gate key and I'll come back whenever it dries up and finish off.'

She's horrified. He'll come back *whenever* he feels like it? Any time. Perhaps one day next week?

'I hope you don't mind,' she says, 'but now that you've nearly finished, I'd like to revert to keeping the side gate locked. So instead of coming anyway in the morning, even if it's raining, could you stay at home and phone me to let me know when you'll be in? Then, when you arrive, I'll open the gate.'

'Oh,' he says. 'OK.'

The next morning it's raining hard. She looks through the curtains.

There's absolutely no sign of him. She relaxes and eats a leisurely breakfast reading the paper. Then she wanders into the sitting room to open the shutters.

He's there painting the railings in the rain.

She goes out. 'I thought you were going to phone.'

'Only if I didn't come first thing, which I did.'

He's lying. She knows he's lying.

'I know when you arrived,' she says.

She's lying. He knows she's lying.

'Really,' he says.

She doesn't open the side gate.

A little later the window cleaners arrive. She can hear him telling them that they can't clean the windows because the paint needs to harden. They look put out. God, she thinks, it's been hardening for five weeks.

'It's a nightmare,' he says to them. 'I can't get in to finish my work. The side gate's locked.' He bangs on the window and gestures at her.

She frowns, pretending not to understand. He gestures again.

She puts her head out. 'Can I help?'

'The key,' he says. 'I need to get in.'

She opens the gate.

'Nearly finished?' she says breezily.

'Yes, but before I make out the bill, I expect you'd like me to run through what I've done.'

'No thanks,' she says. 'It's fine. Really.'

'I'll bring the bill round later on then.'

'Oh no, please don't go to any trouble. Just post it,' she smiles.

'It's no bother,' he says.

And then he's gone.

She sleeps the sleep of the reprieved and wakes fresh, pulls open the curtains, showers, dresses and wanders happily to and fro looking for her hairbrush. She doesn't remember leaving it on the dressing table in the spare room. But there it is. She sits down, smiling at her reflection in the mirror and picks up the brush. And that's when she sees the mass of sandy hairs.

NANCY LEE

We Three Kings

IT STRUCK Marcus that somehow, in the allotment of assets, Diane had managed to get Christmas. Living room mantel strewn with cedar bows, crystallised fruit in glass vases, a tree in the corner near the largest window, where Marcus had never wanted it, lit with candles instead of lights, which he had never allowed. And, as if Diane had arranged them herself, a nativity of old friends. Marcus waved from the entryway.

Diane's surprise had stiffened into a paint-peeling glare, a staple of their failed marriage. 'You really are a shit, you know that?' The baby smallness of her bottom teeth, her rigid back, the thrill of her anger: spoils for the uninvited.

He smiled as she helped Tish out of her coat. The girl's backless gunmetal dress rendered Diane's floor-length skirt, rabbit's paw of cream angora, dowdy and marmish. Diane glowered. He pictured her later that night, standing by the ensuite sink in her slip, mouth full of minty foam as she mocked Tish with a wiggle of her hips and a wave of her toothbrush, another man's laughter from the bed; the effort of smiling ached in Marcus's jaw.

He guided Tish into the party, hand on her warm, bare skin, her muscles tensing beneath his touch. Women at this age reminded him of wild dogs, ribs showing, vigilant and vicious; languorous alone, unpredictable in a pack.

The air hung ripe with cinnamon and cloves, a pre-pubescent choir keened the *Messiah*, strewn pine cones, loops of velvet ribbon; with Diane it was always overkill. He looked to Tish for a dose of disdain. She had a habit of criticising everything, misinformed arrogance, the blessed snobbery of youth.

'It's beautiful.' She blinked at him, her cheeks still red from the cold.

He steered her to the drinks table, nodded and smiled at Jackie and Tom, Elsa and Bradley, Mortimer and Lyle, their adopted son, Rupert; sucked breath through his teeth as he spotted Ali-Hamzah: Gucci corpulence filling an antique armchair. Ali-Hamzah, as if smelling him in the room, turned slowly, nose in the air, and scowled. Marcus had run into him a week before at Starbucks. Ali-Hamzah, bejewelled tide sweeping back from the United Arab Emirates, body doubled by a puffy jacket, had almost suffocated Marcus in his embrace. The big man's ebullient and fortuitous RSVP assured he hadn't been told of the separation. That someone had since enlightened Ali-Hamzah was evidenced by the thousand torturous deaths his eyes now conveyed.

Marcus ladled a glass of punch for Tish. She held it to her lips, her gaze wide, scoping. He poured two bourbons, downed them in fiery succession, then poured a third, anchoring glass, scanned the room for the Gimp.

Diane had told Marcus about Jameson, but only after Marcus had pressed her. Friends, their hijacked loyalties, hushed hostage voices, conceded Jameson by name, but never affliction. From the internet, Marcus deciphered the withered chump would be in a chair, might have use of his upper body, probably took Viagra. Half man, half shopping cart, the lucky feeb had wheeled in for the rebound.

And proposed. Diane mentioned it casually at the lawyers' office, as if men proposed to her every day. The house not even out of escrow. The question of whether Jameson fucked like normal kept Marcus awake at night.

Marcus had a clear view of the living room, dining room and kitchen. No glint of metal, no rubber wheels. Perhaps Diane had come to her senses, locked him in the attic.

He shepherded Tish through the kitchen crowd, stopped twice to speak to huddles of ex-friends, their vacuous questions drifting like sand across a desert. Their eyes scraped over Tish. She insisted on saying, 'So nice to meet you,' shaking hands with each of them.

At the sink, armed with paring knives, the two Russian babushkas Diane always hired for parties, heads down, KGB eyes flitting, gauging his presence. Diane marched in from the hallway, body sheathed in a clingy red dress that opened wide across her shoulders, showed the points of her collarbone. Marcus straightened, breath rushing into him. The bourbon spread its heated roots. She stopped at the sink to wash her hands. 'You've changed!' The babushkas erect, perplexed. Diane shrugged and waved them off.

Marcus winked at Tish. She giggled, swayed, sipped her punch, her tongue flicking the rim of her glass. Something buzzed. She dug into her purse, held up her phone. 'It's Debbie. I better take it.'

'Sure.' He held her gaze to show how the constant irritation of calls and texts from her network of co-dependent girlfriends slid easily from his burnished self-confidence.

In the hallway, a crowd hovered at the study entrance. He swirled the bourbon in his glass, tried not to watch Diane garnish canapés, sauntered to the study instead.

Inside the warm, leathered room, the Gimp. Parked in the

centre of the carpet, younger and rougher than Marcus had imagined, dress shirt taut over an impressive upper body, shoulders and arms like pythons mating. Standing room only, couch, armchair, floor space, doorway crammed with audience.

'– felt so bad when they found me, legs dangling out of their front seat, it didn't even occur to them to call the cops.'

The crowd laughed. Cropped goatee, self-deprecating grin, an open, welcoming face. Marcus had to lean to the side to even see the chair, smaller, and lower than he had guessed. Jameson's trousers sagged around his thighs, withered down his calves. Marcus allowed himself the luxury of staring. Jameson launched back into his story, the crowd captive. 'This other time, the cops –'

Sensing his gaze, the woman in front of Marcus looked back over her shoulder. 'He tried breaking into cars as an act of rebellion against his injury.' Her wine-soaked whisper.

Marcus raised his eyebrows. 'Oh, is that all?' Walked away.

The kitchen had cleared except for Diane, arranging tartlets on a tray, and the two babushkas, counting out tiny forks. From the living room, Lyle's first chords at the piano as he warmed up for his insipid repertoire of yuletide jazz.

Marcus leaned against the counter. 'I need to talk to you.'

'Your girlfriend's looking for you.'

'It's important.'

'I'm busy.'

He pointed to one of the babushkas. 'Take over, please?'

The babushka tucked her chin, slipped in beside Diane.

'For Christ's sake, Marc, I have a house full of people.' Her voice already shaky, the stress of his ambush overwhelming amidst the pressure of entertaining.

144

He tried not to smile. 'We'll go outside.' Before she could protest, he strode to the guest room, fished two coats from the bed pile: a long, elegant white wool with a fox collar, a black overcoat for himself. He returned to the kitchen, coats as an offering. Face stony, she snatched the black coat, pulled it over herself as she pushed out the back door. They stood in the shadowed far corner of the deck, the kitchen window a bright eye, a craning babushka its wary pupil. The white coat bound like a harness, his shoulders hitched, arms rigid in the tube sleeves, fur tickling his chin and ears. Diane patted her coat's oversized pockets, dug inside, pulled out a soft pack of American cigarettes, an enormous silver lighter. She tapped the pack, put one to her lips. Her face smooth and unworried in the flame's light.

'You don't smoke.'

'What do you know?' She took a long, open-lipped draw.

'How have you been?'

'Is this the important conversation?'

His eyes adjusted. He could see her jaw's tiny pulses as she chewed at herself, a nervous habit that left the sides of her mouth raw and bloody, lent her kisses a curious taste.

'I've been thinking.' His arms felt ridiculous. He forced his hands into the coat's tight pockets, felt a tear of stitches on each side.

She stared at the orange tip of her cigarette, jaw still busy, turned her body away from him. He wanted to reach for her elbow, but the pockets had seized down on his wrists. He stepped towards her. 'I was thinking we could still have them. I mean, make them. Together. And share them. You, me and what's his name. I mean, come on, let's face it, you're probably not going to get any out of him. And well, I'd like to have them, too. It seems such a waste to just throw away all those years, and have nothing to show for it. It's not like we didn't plan to have kids, we just never got around to it. So it really wouldn't be any different than if we'd had them before all this. I mean, not really.' He waited, the cold biting its way in, down his neck, up his pant legs.

Diane shivered.

'All I'm saying is we still could.'

She whipped around. 'Are you insane?' Her cigarette hand butted his chest, a hard, jarring punch. 'Are you? Are you?' She thudded him over and over. 'Because if you are, then I can feel sorry for you.'

He wrenched his hands from the coat, grabbed her arms. 'We're going to be divorced, do you understand that?' The words seethed out of him. Her arms slackened. He let them slip from his grasp.

She shook her head. 'You're.' A huff of breath clouded her face. 'Unbelievable.' She stared at him.

He warmed himself in her gaze, comfortable now that her narrow rage had found its target.

'You. Left. Me.'

His voice cooled into a familiar place. 'And you let me.'

She rolled her eyes. Her insolence sent a charge through him.

'You never once begged me to stay, you know that?'

Diane crushed her cigarette on the deck rail. 'Is that what it takes to get rid of you, Marc? A twenty-one-gun salute, a fucking parade?' She stalked back to the house.

He hadn't expected an abrupt ending. She seemed to have less and less patience for him. As a combatant, she had once been inexhaustible. Now, he had to stoke her with ploys, inflammatory statements chiselled and perfected in the grey hours before dawn.

He yanked off the coat, lining stitches popping, left it slumped on the frosted deck, wandered in circles. The cold gnawed him alive, barbs of a premature finish prickled his stomach.

He crossed to the dining-room window, watched Diane glide in, all tinsel and fairy lights, clap her hands together to signal the beginning of games.

As people arranged themselves into competing teams, he caught sight of Tish. The poor girl teetered on the arm of Ali-Hamzah's chair, held her punch glass in both hands, spoke to no one.

He let himself back into the empty kitchen, veered away from the shuffling bodies, eager to avoid Diane's Christmas veneer, the Gimp's prowess at pass-the-parcel or yuletide trivia. Bad as he felt for Tish, she'd have to come find him.

He wandered the empty hallway, tried to remember which photographs had hung in frames there. Tried to picture the dark olive paint he had argued against, now a gutless, sensible cream. The alcove shelf on to which they had once tossed mail and keys, converted into a recessed Zen fountain, steady dribbles of water like a leaking wound.

The study, dark and abandoned, shades drawn, lights off. He closed the door, felt his way to the leather couch. He had been saving the joint for later, for when he and Tish got down to their underwear, but a puff or two might be all he needed, enough to level off. He lit up and took a short hit.

Laughter from the living room, Elsa's ascending cackle breaking over the din. He rested his face against the cool leather, the smoke and blackness a balm. This room, at least, remained the same. His absence perceptible only in the diminished catalogue of books and CDs. Was it as if he had never been here or as if he'd never left? He couldn't decide.

'You wanna share that?'

He jolted upright, coughed on the smoke in his throat. Felt someone closing in, heard the sound of floating, which made no sense as he thought it. Then in front of him, a dim hand, an arm, the silvery curve of a wheel. Breath shuddered out of him.

'Didn't mean to scare you.' The hand beckoned with a tremor.

Marcus held out the joint.

Jameson clamped it in the space between his thumb and palm, his index finger pointed in the air, his last three digits curled in a permanent fist. He took a long, hard toke, then, without pause, a robust second hit. He spoke in a pinched voice. 'You in here earlier?'

'No.' Marcus reached for the joint, careful not to brush Jameson's claw. He tried for two drags, but could only manage one; his stomach retreated, twisted on itself.

Jameson exhaled slowly. 'You missed a good one.'

Marcus watched the breath like a cartoon, a long, thick snake of smoke. And it made sense then, what Jameson was, a Yosemite Sam, an Elmer Fudd, a Foghorn Leghorn without the legs.

'I could charge for that shit, you know what I'm saying?'

'No.' Marcus raised his legs to the couch, turned on his side, held the joint at his mouth, and sipped, set to keep it all to himself. The claw materialised in front of his face, index finger jerking. Marcus handed it back.

'Her ex is here. How fucked up is that? As if I ain't got enough problems.' Another Olympic draw.

Marcus leaned forward to snatch the joint back. His fingers fumbled against what must have been calluses. The sensation made him nauseous. He could only pretend to toke.

'You know him?'

'No.' He felt lighter for saying it. Like he could lift away, leave them to sort it out. What the fuck could he do anyway? Stop the man from stealing his wife? He couldn't even keep a joint to himself.

'Here.' The claw trembled in the air. 'I'm being a hog.'

Marcus took a relaxed pull, passed the nub back to Jameson. The couch a leather cocoon. Jameson's wheelchair rolled back and forth, a lullaby of berber and mechanics. 'I love your chair.'

Jameson laughed. Pursed his lips at the joint, then waved his hand. 'I'm gonna eat this if you don't mind.'

'Knock yourself out.' He watched Jameson's hand at his mouth, a giant baby sucking its thumb. Marcus raised his own thumb to his lips, but resisted the urge. 'I hear you're getting married.'

The chair rolled again. 'I asked her. But she hasn't said one way or the other. I figure, if they don't answer right away, that's not a good sign, right?' The room full of the chair's sweet brushing. Jameson waiting for an answer.

Fuck you, buddy, was all Marcus could think.

The chair stopped. 'Well, I better get back before she starts looking for me.' The chair glided to the door. Light from the hallway seared, and Marcus turned his face into the back of the couch, limbs too heavy to move.

Marcus caught Tish as she stepped out of the bathroom, her skin glowing, glossed mouth slipping into a troubled line. She pulled the door closed behind her with an emphatic snap. 'You really know how to treat a girl.' She'd done something to her hair, it tendrilled wildly around her face.

149

'I'm an ass.' He cupped her waist, settled her against the door, nuzzled her ear, her skin damp and hot. 'You should hate me for ever.'

Her face remained turned, but her body softened, the flush of anger fading from her cheeks and neck. Her hand settled on his arm, kneaded the fabric of his suit jacket. 'You missed all the fun.' She looked up at him, pupils wide with injury.

He mimicked her sullen bottom lip, then shook his head. 'We'll make our own.'

Her hand shifted to his chest, played with the buttons of his shirt. 'Did you watch today?' She was a disciple of afternoon television psychology.

'I had a meeting.'

'Oh, it was so good.' She lowered her head and nodded in reverence. 'It was about relationships and that story, the Gift of the Magi. You know that one?'

'Mm-hm.' He prayed she wouldn't retell it.

She pressed against him, her breath sugary and alcoholic. 'It's like, when we're in a relationship, we're the magi, wandering the desert with nothing but faith to guide us, and we're each carrying our own special gift. Except our gifts are ourselves, you see?' She touched herself, fingers circling the rise of her breast.

'I see.' His hands traced her hips, trailed to her ass, felt the ridge of her g-string beneath the silky fabric.

'I think I'm frankincense, what do you think?' She pushed her pubis into him.

'Sure.'

'And you're –' She squinted as she examined his face. 'Oh my God, Marky Marc, are you high?'

He shrugged.

'You pig.' Her body rocked against his. 'Didn't your mommy teach you to share?'

'Guess not.'

'I was going to say you were gold, but now you're just myrrh.' She tucked her chin in a fake sulk.

'Myrrrrrrh.' The word growled up in his throat. He shifted his leg so his stiffness ground against her.

She giggled, stepped away, tugged at his hand. 'Come on, they're playing charades.'

He nodded. 'Just a sec. I need to use the facilities.'

Her mouth slipped into a pout. 'You've left me alone all night.'

'I'll be quick. You can wait if you want.'

She looked over her shoulder at the bathroom door, her brow crinkled like a candy wrapper. She squeezed his thumb. 'Come find me.'

He watched her walk away, admired the prowling roll of her hips.

The bathroom door had always been tricky, an ancient brass fitting that yielded on its own accord. He twisted back and forth, rattled, twisted again, until a man's cough startled his hand from the knob.

'Sorry! Sorry!' Ali-Hamzah's singsong voice echoed into the hall. 'Occupied!'

Marcus leaned in the living-room doorway. Bourbon glow faded to a raw alcohol scour, the veil of pot more fuzz than lift, he watched the room watch Diane as she patted three fingers to the inside of her elbow.

'Jurassic!'

'Concubine!'

Diane frenzied her team-mates along, ecstatic smile, hands waving.

Jameson hunkered near the Christmas tree, forearms wrapped in black braces that allowed him to hold a water

151

glass in one hand, an open bottle of Jim Beam in the other. Tish sat on an ottoman, chin in her palm, half laughing at the game, half peering back at Marcus, face puppyish with apology.

'Prostitute? Call girl?'

Time to go. Only, he wanted to take Diane with him. Fold her, pack up her painful posture, weak teeth, debilitating stubbornness, her middle-of-the-night little-girl voice and hurry them back to his empty apartment.

'American Gigolo!'

'Yes!' Diane punched two fists in the air. The clatter of applause.

Ali-Hamzah appeared in the dining room, set to slow grazing at the buffet table. Fat fingers delivered pinches of food to his pursed mouth. His hands moved hungrily, but his eyes stayed on Tish. Tish blushed and shifted in her seat.

Someone in the crowd called for Jameson to take a turn. Jameson shook his head, tipped bottle to glass. A round of childish name chanting: Ja-me-son, Ja-me-son. Marcus stepped back into the hallway.

Diane had redone the master suite in taupes, light and dark, a gritty beige carpet, and, everywhere, fabrics like layered skins, all of them stony non-colours. Marcus fingered the rough silk bedspread, a velveteen pillow, crossed the room to the dressing table.

From her jewellery box, he picked out the cloisonné bracelet he'd bought in Hong Kong, the pear-shaped diamond pendant he'd chosen extravagantly, resentfully, last Christmas, earrings, a watch, two strings of pearls, a Celtic locket and, as he held his breath, her engagement ring and wedding band. From her lingerie drawer, he took a familiar blue teddy, a silk camisole that had been his favourite, three pairs of sheer panties. Stuffed it all into his pockets. Laughter burbled from the living room, then bursts of cheers, raucous victory, the game disbanding. He looked to the half-closed door. If anyone dared poke their head in, he'd show them what was rightfully his.

The closet. Diane's span of dated clothes punctuated by a cluster of men's shirts, stripes and checks, limp trousers in a row. He tore the trousers from their hangers, wadded them into balls and hurled them into the back corner of the closet. A tangled and useless pile of legs.

'Oh, for God's sake.' Jameson's voice drew close.

Marcus tucked himself behind the closet's bi-fold door.

'Just get off my fucking case.' Jameson rolled in, rocked back and forth, his forearms bare, the plush carpet like sand slowing his wheels. The bedroom door clicked shut.

'Keep your voice down.' Diane came around to the front of Jameson's chair, knelt at his feet. Marcus heard only the short, hollow huffs of his own breath. Diane's long, sturdy hand on Jameson's ankle, and for a second, she rested her head on his knee. Marcus swallowed against hardness in his throat. Jameson sat stiff, eyes glazed and unfocused.

She smoothed his pant leg, fingered the hem, then folded the cuff slowly up his calf. A plastic bag strapped to Jameson's leg, liquid the colour of weak tea. Marcus wiped his eyes.

'It's still cloudy. Did you start the antibiotics?'

'It's a fucking party, Di.'

She yanked the pant leg down. 'You just hate me, is that it?'

'I'm trying to have a good time.' Jameson stared at the carpet, chin lolling.

'For God's sake, you can barely sit up.'

Jameson shrugged. 'I told you. One of your friends –'

Diane threw up her hands.

'He practically forced it on me.'

'My friends don't do that shit, Jamie. My friends are adults.'

Jameson banged his arm against the wheel of his chair. 'What the fuck am I then?' He struggled to sit himself straight. 'Is that what you're doing here, Di? Being mommy because I can't make wee wee in the potty?'

Marcus winced. He watched Diane blink, her jaw gnawing frustration. 'I can't talk to you when you're like this.'

'What? Paralysed?'

'Yes, of course. The excuse for everything.' Diane stared at her fingernails.

Jameson wheeled his chair so that his back was to her. Silence. Marcus could hear the carpet brush beneath his shoes. When Jameson spoke, Marcus had to concentrate to make out the words. 'Why did you invite him?'

Diane's face slackened. 'I didn't invite him. He barged in.'

'You didn't stop him.' Jameson nodded, his torso unsteady with the motion. 'I guess it's hard to resist, that feeling of someone wanting you.' He stilled himself. 'Not that I would know.'

Diane's skin began to colour, a flush creeping up from her neck. She crossed her arms at her stomach, held herself, then stretched out a hand to touch Jameson's chair, fingers tracing the cushioned back, her thumb kneading it gently. She knelt again, her body soft, fluid. Marcus crouched down with her. Her hand settled on Jameson's belt.

'Just stop fucking –' Jameson leaned to the side. 'Don't touch me.'

'I should check the catheter.' Her voice hushed and watery as she stood. 'We need to change the bag.'

Marcus willed Jameson to turn and look at her, but instead he twisted his body away. 'I'll do it. Later.'

'It's easier when I do it.'

'Well, la-di-fucking-da for you.'

'Just let me help you.' She reached for his buckle.

Jameson's arm flailed out. A sharp, stinging smack in the air. Diane recoiled, wrist clutched to her chest. Jameson raised his head. Each of them wide-eyed and motionless, as if shocked by the sight of the other. Marcus couldn't breathe. Diane shook her head, mouth agape, eyes wet. 'Go fuck yourself then. Go fucking fuck yourself.' She sat on the bed and cried into her palms, thin, high notes, small hiccups of despair. Jameson cradled his guilty arm, shoulders trembling.

Marcus sniffled. The closet squeezed at his back. Beyond the bedroom window, winter's dark, unguided path. His hands churned and tangled inside his pockets. He raised them up, and, in the thin cut of light, stared at the sheen of silk, the pearls' milky lustre, facets and glimmers of jewels and gold. With a shivering breath, he stepped forward, baring all his useless gifts.

PATRICIA DUNCKER

Doubling Up

I MUST DRESS carefully. Dark clothes, my solicitor advised, low heels, a navy suit, straight skirt, not trousers. No jewellery. I have to look sober, wronged. This is my first court appearance. It isn't a trial, simply a preliminary hearing in chambers. No gowns, no wigs. But we will be obliged to do all that, all the dressing up, for the divorce – my two minutes of glory in a real courtroom. The gallery will probably be empty, unless the journalists snatch up the affair again. I have never been so publicly humiliated. It is bad enough that my husband has betrayed me, worse that he may go to prison, but having the details of our hidden lives splattered all over the tabloid headlines – I cannot bear that. My marriage is over. I intend to divorce my husband.

We lived in a small, quiet northern town where the mills had closed down, and the buildings been recycled into big franchise chains, Carpet Right, Halfords, Tesco; all the old, local industries gathered up and packed away. Everyone travelled to work in Manchester or Sheffield. I filled in as a receptionist at the local surgery – bunions, back pain, the 'Give It Up' Smokers' Clinic – making careful distinctions between attention-seeking hysteria and desperate emergencies. I counted on quiet in my life, a steady symmetry of days where nothing changed. My husband was a driver on the railways. He was often away during the week and I learned to enjoy my solitude. When we were first married we hoped for children. I endured three miscarriages in rapid succession. The disappointment proved intolerable and so we settled for a golden retriever called Sally. We called the first one Sally. And the second. The third Sally lies asleep at my feet. We never changed the name, not because we lacked imagination, but because I hated change. We redecorated the lounge in the same colours every few years. And I struggled to find the same shade of orange for the sofa's renewed cushions. My husband built a summerhouse in the garden to mark our tenth wedding anniversary and our tenth year in the same house. My husband wanted us to eat dinner by candlelight in the fragile pagoda – to celebrate. I persuaded him to remain at the dining-room table. We left the curtains open so that we could see the illuminated summerhouse balanced above the rockery. I liked looking at the white trellis, gleaming in the gloom, but I had no desire to carry hot food across a damp lawn. Some people thought I was the conventional partner in our marriage, but of the two of us, my husband was the steady one. He used to say, 'I like things as they are. Why should we live differently, or make changes, just for the hell of it? No, stay the way you are, my love, stay just the way you are.'

If you treasure quiet, calm and uneventful continuity in your daily world, the unexpected and the tragic do not erupt, completely unexpected, into your tranquil existence. You know that anything can happen. But you hide that knowledge at the bottom of your mind. You fear the unexpected phone call, the knock upon the door. And of course the time came for me, as it does for all of us. But it wasn't the police, or a community counsellor. Here comes my next-door neighbour, barging through the gate, leaning on the bell. She had switched on the six o'clock news and seen the first footage of the accident – a passenger train smashed head-on into a goods convoy on the branch line between Shrewsbury and Welshpool. We stare at torn metal horror and sheeted bodies; one carriage lies on its side, still smoking gently.

'Didn't you say Len drove that line?'

'He does. But it can't be him. The accident happened at nine twenty this morning. I've been in all day and I've had no messages, no calls. They let the wives know first.'

'Try his mobile.'

I did. Len urges me cheerfully to leave him a message.

'He switches it off when he's driving. That's the regulation.'

'I'm getting my knickers in a twist about nothing then. Of course they'd have rung you by now. Awful though, isn't it? Two people dead and dozens in hospital. I haven't felt safe on trains since Potter's Bar.'

And that night, despite finishing all my usual tasks – red plastic number on the doorstep for our milkman, walk Sally twice, up round the water troughs, back past The Marquis of Bath and down the hedged lane, scour the sink, pop a little bit of bleach in the downstairs loo, add bird seed to the shopping list, cut down the flowers, throw out the dead ones, put them in the kitchen where it's cooler, turn off the TV standby so that the red eye fades – nothing was unusual, out of the ordinary, yet I felt terribly anxious, unsafe. I left another message on my husband's mobile. He was on night shift and still not answering. I took comfort in that. When the accident occurred he would have been at his digs in Shrewsbury. I sent him a loving text. We have matching phones; he bought them both and arranged our numbers one digit apart. He always replies with another text, every night, no matter how late it is, and the sound of the beep as my mobile catches his returning text and holds it safe is usually the last thing that I hear before morning. Sometimes I get up and read the message, sometimes I save it – as the first thing he says to me next day.

I wake at 2 a.m. in complete silence. What can I hear? Only the retriever snuffling near the door, a faint wind outside. Nothing. I snatch up the mobile. My husband has not replied. For the first time in eighteen years he has not said goodnight.

My head cleared in alarm. I scuttled downstairs, lunged for the telephone and prepared to ring every hospital in Shrewsbury. I had to spell out his name carefully, twice. And then I heard the bland voice of the night watch replying.

'Yes. He's still in intensive care. No visitors apart from close family.'

'I'm coming. Tell him I'm coming. I'm his wife.'

I never drive at night. I cannot fix the white lines on the side of the road. I am afraid of the cat's-eyes, glowing green and malicious, stretching out before me. But on that night I hurtled down all the lanes and motorways into total darkness, fearless in search of my husband. I was at Shrewsbury General by 4 a.m., standing before the woman who had answered the telephone. And this was the first time that I received any hint that I was not confronting a tragic catastrophe that we would eventually overcome, but the end of my safe world.

'You're his wife? You can't be. She's just left. She's been here for twelve hours. The night staff sent her home to get some rest. So who are you?'

I did not see her that night, or in the days that followed.

The police took me home and my good neighbour, white-faced in the pale morning, came to sit with me until the tranquillisers took hold. My husband is locked up in intensive care at a strange hospital, miles away. And he has another wife. She is not his mistress, or his girlfriend, but his lawful wedded wife and he has lived with her, in a quiet street, not unlike our own, for years and years and years. I watched my calm, stable home and precious household objects – crockery, curtains, bedspreads, all my tended surfaces swilling away into nothingness, as if they had been chewed up by the waste disposal unit. The police were more preoccupied with the accident, not the driver's two marriages. When I felt able to face my husband, months later, he was no longer able to face me.

I contacted the same solicitors who had completed the legal work on our house purchase eighteen years before. The partner who knew us had retired and died, but here sat a spruce new lawyer, a woman with a crisp blonde bob, a prominent nose and dark-rimmed glasses.

'I want a divorce.'

'So does she,' said the lawyer, 'only she doesn't actually need one. I have a copy of her marriage certificate here and it post-dates your marriage.'

'Her marriage?'

'He married her, I'm afraid. She thinks she really is his wife. But she isn't. You are.'

Mine was the older marriage, and the deeper betrayal.

'I want a divorce!' My rage suddenly reached full volume.

Then the papers got wind of a great new angle on the train crash. TWICE-WED LEN DRIVES DEATH EXPRESS. And the worst things began to emerge. In the illicit photographs procured from the back of their house I spotted the summer pergola, the pretty white trellis attached to the rose-covered garden pavilion, the one he had built for her. I caught a glimpse of their hallway wallpaper: dark green covered in tiny yellow roses, the same paper we had in our hall. And the nightmare reached a horrible crescendo when the London journalist, backed by a photographer, doorstepped me in a defenceless moment. Sally rushed out barking and I dragged her back.

'Good God,' yelled the journalist, 'he's got two golden retrievers named Sally!'

The headlines read: BIGAMY! MAKE IT A CRIME.

'It is a crime,' spat my solicitor, grim-faced, 'but we'll have to wait until the initial inquiry into the rail crash is complete.'

She stared, curious, at the photographs of his two homes. The other woman's family had whisked her off to Scotland, away from the floodlights of scandal. There were no photographs of her, and only a blurred one of me pushing Sally back through the front door. But the evidence was eerie, disturbing. He was fond of home building works and had used all the same wood, paper, pelmets, beading, paint. The two houses were identical.

'Well,' declared my barrister, 'he obviously wasn't expressing the two sides of his personality.'

I collapsed in tears.

And then I began to dread meeting her, this other woman, who had stolen my identity. They say men always look for a younger version of the woman they married, and indeed, observing the wreckage of my colleagues' lives, I fear that this is true. Had he just wanted to live through our marriage again with the youth and passion comfortably renewed? Did he want the possibility of children once more upon the table? Or was he simply afraid of being alone during his nights away? I heard my own voice wailing, that pathetic bleat with all the things other women say when they are betrayed. What did I do that made you cease to love me? Why wasn't I enough for you? Why did you need her too?

I dare not look up. I know she is here. A tentative rustle stirs the room. The lawyers are rummaging in their papers, curious. For this is the first time the two wives have ever been together in the same place. If I look up I shall see the other woman who has destroyed my life. Everyone is waiting. Someone is coming towards me across the dark carpet. I look up.

And before me stands a dumpy middle-aged woman in a navy suit. She has short grey hair, as I do. She is clutching an unused handbag with a gold clasp, no jewellery. I am looking into the mirror with the same intensity that once gripped the evil queen and I see, not Snow White, but my own ageing face. Her ankles are thickening, her dark laced shoes impeccable. I rise, unsteady, uncertain, overjoyed. I could not have borne a younger face. I have not been displaced. She is already part of me and we are his wives, his two identical wives. I hold out my hand to greet her hesitating smile.

RACHEL CUSK

Thirst

ARRIVING IN Venice the Gibsons – mother and daughter
– were inexplicably startled by the omnipresence of
water. Julia Gibson had concerned herself too much with
the practicalities of the trip; her daughter Charlotte too
little. It was a sort of fashion, in their circle of friends, for a
mother to take a brief holiday of this sort alone with her
oldest child, particularly if she was a girl and pubescent; as
though it were the subject of general agreement that these
two family members required special consideration and
privileges, whether to mollify or reward them it was un-
clear. Julia and Charlotte were spending three nights away,
which vaguely seemed the correct number to satisfy either
requirement. It might have been this air of diplomatic
import that caused the character of their destination to
recede, as businessmen and politicians were said to zigzag
around the globe without ever quite knowing where they
were. They could have been going anywhere: the airplane
itself, for example, seemed both neutral and unaccustomed
enough for their vague and ominous purposes. It was some
time since Julia Gibson had last troubled the world for
anything: mostly she forgot that it was there. It did not seem
unreasonable to her, strapped to her seat in the dry blue
parabola of the heavens, that she should choose now to
descend on it. Here and there the sky was streaked with

white; the stealthy tracks of other aircraft, which gave the sky a used and somehow dishonourable look, as though the marks were the evidence of a whole subterfuge of business and pleasure that went on indifferent to the drama below.

At the airport it seemed they were expected to board a boat, and it was there, rising and falling riotously on the choppy waters with their cheeks red from half an hour of waiting on the shifting wooden pontoon in the cold fresh maritime evening, that the singularity of their predicament made itself known to Julia and her daughter.

'If Daddy had had his way we'd be in Madrid!' Julia cried out over the noise of the engine, grasping Charlotte's arm in its padded coat sleeve whose slippery material resisted her fingers. 'Do you know what I think? I think he didn't want us to have too much fun.'

She often spoke in this way to the children about their father. It was a means of disclosing, to them or to herself, the site of an injury she had borne, not unwillingly, for the sake of them all. In the privacy of her maternal world she lifted her garment and displayed her scar, the seam of her cortated self which retained areas of numbness and, still, of unpredictable tenderness. It was true that he had suggested they go to Madrid. He hadn't seemed able to explain why he had. He said he thought they would enjoy it, that was all. Julia had never been to Madrid, but the taint of its availability told her everything she needed to know about it. There were several possibilities: one was that he actually didn't want them to have too much fun; another – not unrelated – was that he wanted to go to Venice himself; another, draughtier possibility was that he was right.

'Do you think you'd have preferred to go to Madrid?'

She clutched Charlotte's arm again and pumped it up and down against the cold. The cold was imaginary – the boat was heated inside – but Charlotte's physical passivity often aroused her in this way.

'I don't know,' Charlotte said. 'I don't know what it's like. It depends.'

'Well, I think it's very *interesting*,' Julia said, furrowing her brow as though with an effort of exceptional sincerity. 'I think there are lots of museums and, you know, *public buildings*, monuments and that kind of thing. I think it's a great administrative centre.'

Charlotte said nothing.

'Whereas Venice –' Julia gestured with her hand towards the window, through which was visible the fortuitous pink light of dusk over the lagoon, 'Venice is a magical place, a fairytale place. It's unique. It's like going back to visit the past. Did you know there aren't any cars in Venice? Not a single one!'

'Why not?' Charlotte looked concerned, as though the absence of cars were disadvantageous and sinister.

'Because there aren't any roads! Instead they have canals. You remember about the canals. I told you about them.'

'No, you didn't.'

'Darling,' said Julia severely, 'I did.'

'Is this it?' Charlotte said presently, roused by the slowing effortful vibrations of the engine.

A great bank of stone buildings radiant with electric light had silently manifested itself to one side of the boat, set back from the water. The big inscrutable facades of hotels succeeded one another all along the seafront. On top of one of the buildings tall hoardings spelled the word CAMPARI.

'Anyway, there *are* cars,' Charlotte observed.

Little pairs of headlights sped up and down beside them making spiky orange shapes in the gloom. There was traffic on the water too. A huge olive-coloured ferry trawled past them and headed out to sea. Half the people on the boat stood up and began to file towards the door with their bags and coats. The conductor shouted something.

'This is Venice Lido,' Julia said decidedly. 'It isn't Venice itself. Lido is a sort of resort. It has a famous beach.'

'So why doesn't everyone just come here instead?' said Charlotte, with the archness that her mother particularly detested because it was undeniably the area of life in which Charlotte expended the most effort.

Julia was silent until their boat had crossed the dark lagoon to Venice and they could see it standing like a golden crown on the black water. She was silent as they passed the Arsenale with its compact shadowy masses of trees, and the first bridges like little frowns over the probing canals. She was silent even as they glided past the spectacle of what she guessed from her reading to be St Mark's Square lit up in the darkness, and the cornucopia of the Doge's Palace, and the gold pate of the basilica, feeling that Charlotte would profit from the opportunity to become thoroughly mystified before Julia need take it upon herself to enlighten her any further. Wooden moorings stood everywhere out of the water in thick bundles and amidst them ranks of tethered gondolas floated, most of them covered in tight tarpaulins; a precaution, she supposed, against the January night, or an indication of their unseasonality. The sight was both charming and slightly morbid. The boat slowed and hovered, and then taxied in sideways to a little lit-up grey and yellow station with a sign that said *S. Marco*.

'This is it,' Julia said in a wistful tone, as though they had arrived at a place where she had already lived a whole life, a life that had recently and grievously come to an end. She rose from her plastic seat and made her way down the boat with their suitcase. After a long hesitation which she sensed rather than saw, Charlotte got up and followed her.

A friend had told Julia that there was only one place for them to stay in Venice, and although this statement bore some of the inferences of Madrid – its suggestion of Julia as a level at which things could be pitched – she had called and reserved a room there. The friend had seemed surprised that Julia had got in. Normally, she said, you had to reserve months in advance. She concluded that it was the time of year that explained it. They got on another boat, a *vaporetto*, which was much slower and barrelled heavily up the Grand Canal with such a juddering commotion that Julia's enthusiasm was revived as though it had been shaken.

'We're *here*!' she shouted, gripping Charlotte's shoulders; and then, 'This is the Grand Canal – one of the most famous sights in the world!'

'You can't really see it,' Charlotte observed. 'It's too dark.'

'Don't worry,' Julia said, 'we'll be spending our *lives* going up and down it.'

'Will we?'

'Of course we will. Why, were you planning on just staying in the hotel for three days?'

Charlotte shrugged. 'I don't know.'

'You can do that if you want,' said her mother, 'but it would be a shame.'

'Anyway, I couldn't do it,' Charlotte said presently, gazing out through the foggy windows at the black water and the extravagantly gracious form of a church floating by. 'You wouldn't let me.'

'Why would you *want* to?' smiled Julia. 'That's a very strange thing to want to do in Venice, don't you think?'

Only a few months earlier Charlotte would certainly have

responded to this by saying that she hadn't *said* she wanted to; now, however, she merely turned her head, causing her mother to feel a sense of destitution, of a shortfall, that was both troubling and corrective. She became immediately aware of the groomed, brown-eyed glances of the other passengers, to whom the nature of this exchange appeared to be apparent; and for an instant she had the picture of herself flamboyantly clothed in the coarseness of her rela-tionships. Once, years ago, on a family holiday in France, she had seen a woman slap her daughter's cheeks, a girl the age Charlotte was then. The woman was good-looking; so was the daughter, which lent the scene a certain stringent drama.

'Water!' she cried out again, when they were off the *vaporetto* and following the map through the narrow sepulchral streets to the hotel. She ran up the ramp of a small bridge and positioned herself at its apex in the dark, dropping the suitcase in order to fling out her arms over the cold motionless ribbon of a little canal that lay there exuding vapours. She had hoped to make Charlotte laugh, which Charlotte obligingly did. 'Water, water everywhere!' Julia exclaimed, so that muffled figures passing over the bridge turned their heads.

The man at the hotel desk directed them to a *trattoria* which he thought might be open at this time of year, although he couldn't be sure. It will be a good sign if it is, he said mysteriously.

Three times during the night Julia woke with a sensation of physical urgency, which each time she was surprised to recognise as tremendous thirst. Again and again she rose and went unsteadily through the darkness of their room with its obscure forms of furniture, to stand in the harsh light of the little bathroom and drink water. On the way back, not driven now by need, she was able each time to look at Charlotte asleep in the other bed and to feel a yearning for her which the object of Charlotte herself failed to satisfy; which, if anything, she actually intensified by having supplanted the version of Charlotte in which the roots of Julia's love and knowledge lay. In the morning Charlotte claimed that she too had made numerous journeys in search of water, which seemed incredible, when Julia had traversed the night like a sentry and never once noticed her daughter even stir. It appeared that Charlotte's night had occurred separately from Julia's, in some parallel, autonomous universe of incipient adulthood. In the little breakfast room that looked out over the garden and where Julia was brought coffee and milk in heavy silver jugs in whose sides her distorted image wavered, the Gibsons obliquely examined the other guests. There was a slender elderly gentleman with a brown lined face, dressed in a dark blue suit. With him sat a young boy who wore an expression of benign politeness and whose dark hair was brushed so that it lay neatly flattened back from his face. They conversed in heavily accented English. By the window sat a large, middle-aged couple who ate steadily without speaking. There was also a family – two adults, two small shiny-haired children – who smiled and smiled, at each other and at everyone else.

'I think the food must have been very salty,' Charlotte said.

'I suppose it might have been,' Julia said. 'I don't know.'

'It was. They must have put so much salt in it.'

'Why do you think that man and his grandson are speaking in English when neither of them *are* English?'

Charlotte looked them over glancingly and shrugged.

'Maybe he's not his grandson,' she said.

'Well, what else would he be?'

'What does it do to you if you have too much salt?'

Julia noticed that Charlotte had gathered her hair into a bunch beside her ear, so that it stuck out from the side of her head like a spigot. She was wearing a little turquoise ring on a thin silver chain around her neck and a heavy metallic bracelet that slid around on her wrist and banged repeatedly against the watch Julia and David had given her. Her large imperturbable eyes were fronded with blue mascara. Her concern with the deleterious effects of salt seemed visibly to rattle and ricochet around the taut walls of the mind behind them. Julia felt a new comprehension forcing itself on her, that in this business of differentiation, of growing up, it was not Charlotte who was departing but Julia herself; Julia who was increasingly guilty of acts of abandonment, in the matter of the spigot and the mascara and of Charlotte's midriff, which she liked to leave exposed at all times so that this tender, private piece of flesh had taken on an anonymous, public character: it was Julia who was disaffected, with this new, unexpected flourishing of her responsibilities. She had had to learn so much in order to teach her children how to exist, and now the curriculum extended all the way up to the point where her own studies had been interrupted; where questions of self, of her own self, lay neglected and unanswered. She had witnessed numerous examples of how other women dealt with this problem, and none of them encouraged her.

'I don't think it's very good for you,' she said. 'But I feel strangely purified, don't you?'

Gratifyingly, Charlotte seemed to give this assertion concerted thought.

'Maybe,' she said, nodding.

They went to the large public art gallery that was conveniently near their hotel, where Julia found herself by turns costive and pedagogic in her representations to Charlotte of the glories of Italian painting. As a student she had spent a term in Florence studying art, and a pulse still faintly beat through that long, attenuated vein; moreover, it had always been accepted by the family, apparently without effort, not just that art was an interest of hers but that it was actually important, which led her to consider how much else she might have incorporated into the legislature of her children's emergent selves and how painlessly. The number of other people in the gallery – not negligible – was like a shadow cast by the great crowds of the tourist season. She and Charlotte found the central Bellinis and three paintings by Giorgione before confining themselves to the two rooms in which the works of Tintoretto and Veronese were displayed.

'We're not messing around here,' Julia said. 'We're just going straight to the point.'

'Shouldn't we look at everything?' Charlotte enquired, as they walked past whole walls at which Julia did not even glance.

I can't, Julia wanted to say. What she couldn't do – not any more – was squander time on what was merely exploratory or reflective; she couldn't lose herself in the connective tissue, the stems and foliage. She already knew too much about that side of life. She sought only the big blooms, the gold, not because she was vain or insensible but because there was desolation in her heart, and savagery: it was a landscape blackened by the needs of others, in which she had acquired a great knowledge of survival; a sort of volcanic terrain where emotion came in big bangs of hot, violent feeling. That was how it sometimes seemed. Often she felt rather regal, though that too caused her to disdain all but one level of human endeavour.

There was an exhibition of Carpaccio, where Charlotte was taken with a painting called *Il Sogno di Orsola* and Julia found herself detained by one of a series depicting the life of Mary. The painting showed a room in a house where various women were occupied in domestic tasks. A baby – Mary – had just been born and her mother lay in bed, raised on her elbow and looking at the scene with an expression on her face Julia recognised, the expression of someone who has left their own body and been returned to it changed. Charlotte's painting was very beautiful. St Ursula had yellow hair and lay very still and flat in her neat white little bed, in her room that was everything desirable in a room, while a handsome young angel stood and watched her sleeping. Later, in the gift shop, Charlotte bought a bookmark with the image of the angel on it.

They walked around the maze of the city in the perfect pink cold sunlight and encountered the charm of its canals and bridges, its unexpected piazzas and quiet alleys and hidden churches, its atmosphere of monitored decay and of self-knowledge, and Julia found that the sleeve of Charlotte's coat was less slippery when she gripped it so that their talk grew warmer and fitted easily back into its proper setting in the past; and for a while all this beauty distracted Julia from her own creeping feelings of ugliness until it began to transform them too, so that when she caught sight of her own reflection in the little shop windows she saw possibilities and even enigmas there, and in the evening when they returned from their restaurant and met the dapper old gentleman and the boy on the stairs, the old man stood back and bowed cordially and said '*buona sera*' and the boy smiled as though he were pleased.

In the morning there were new people in the breakfast room, an Englishman in his twenties as tall and thick and lush as a shop-bought lily, who wore severely fashionable black-framed glasses and primrose yellow corduroy trousers, and stalked around camply fetching things for his companion, an ancient bald little man in a tweed suit. The smiling family smiled at Julia and Charlotte with the intensity of renewed acquaintance. Charlotte said that she had been up in the night again several times drinking water. Julia had filled a bottle and put it beside her own bed, and over the course of the night drained it to the bottom.

'Lucky you,' Charlotte said. 'I had to get up every time.'

'You can have it tonight.'

'I must have got up about six times.'

'I'll fill it up for you and you can have it by your bed.'

Julia said she thought they might devote the day to Tintoretto, who had lived in Venice all his life and whose works were everywhere around the city. In the Scuola di San Rocco there was a vast room in which he had painted the whole life of Christ on the walls and ceiling. Charlotte's downcast eyes widened over her plate.

Julia said: 'Don't you want to do that?'

There was silence.

'It's just that we looked at paintings yesterday,' Charlotte eventually replied. 'I thought we were going to do something else today.'

'Like what?'

'I don't know. Go to some shops or something.'

Julia's friends held the belief, far more passionately than Julia herself did, that the world was a terrible and dangerous place in which the chance to realise the desires of one's

175

children offered a kind of moral, or perhaps merely emotional, harbour. *Poor Charlotte*, these friends would have said, laughing.

'We didn't come to Venice to go shopping,' Julia said.

She realised in the same instant both that she wanted to shame Charlotte and that Charlotte was not ashamed.

'The shops are just as much a part of it as everything else.'

'What, as much as things that have been here for five centuries?'

'Yes!' exclaimed Charlotte, with a defiant toss of her head. 'It doesn't make things automatically good just because they're old, or because they're paintings by one man.'

Regarding Tintoretto's *Slaughter of the Innocents*, Julia felt confirmed in her belief that the world was no more dangerous or terrible than it ever had been. The building was gloomy, and as cold as a tomb. It was an atmosphere of discouragement that intensified the discovery of the paintings, riotous with life, that covered every wall and ceiling on two floors. Charlotte sat huddled in a chair in her coat and didn't look at anything. Julia took her time, as ebullient with self-satisfaction, as capacious and eager as though she were being fattened up for something, but what? The bodies of the women were so monumental that they seemed almost incapacitated by their own frozen knowledge. Tintoretto had a way of painting their fleshy shoulders slightly askew and their heads turned to one side, as though they were perennially responding to some call on their attention. An answering stature aroused itself in Julia's breast. She looked at the mangled forms of the dead children, their little feet, their limp rounded arms, their soft curly heads. She had loved her children so; and now it sometimes seemed as though that love were a grand expense for which she continued to pay in instalments, a single and increasingly remote instance of indulgence. Yet it was only that in those early days she had not guessed at how far her sincerity would be stretched. She was like an actor in a long-running play, who every night must replicate the same drama and feel the same exhaustion afterwards: it was the fact that it continued to tax her in its repetition that was so perplexing. To feel a melancholic, liquid surge of empathy at their little heads and hands and feet, that was her single trick. Sometimes, by contrast, David made her cry in arguments and it was like some ancient hydraulic event occurring in the bowels of a vast old house; a long, rumbling, catastrophic pause after the tap has been turned on, at the end of which a strenuous trickle of stinging brown water would emerge.

In a shop by the Rialto she bought Charlotte a dolphin made of purple glass, by which Charlotte had claimed to be enchanted. In the busy street, in the pink and blue tints of dusk, beside the big, pale, cold canal where the *vaporetti* drew furrows in the water as though in the surface of milk, their disagreement modulated into a series of quiet and comforting transactions; as though some unpleasant but necessary operation had been performed from which they were both recuperating. Julia had been prepared for the writ of Charlotte's taste to run much wider, but her choice of the dolphin seemed almost like an appeal for Julia's sympathy, or even a commentary on her expectations. How could a girl who coveted a purple dolphin be blamed for anything? Julia bought her a bag of chocolates and a Spanish fan with a picture of St Mark's Square on it, and in a cluttered little shop in a side street they spent an hour looking at painted Venetian masks while outside darkness filled the city as though it sat at the bottom of a well. The shop was warm and dusty and bright with electric light. It smelled of wood and paint. The young Italian woman behind the counter told them that in the past Venetian women used masks not only during Carnival but as a regular tool of mystification. Charlotte lifted one to her face. It had a plume of pink feathers and scrolls of sequins around the eyes.

'What do you think?' she said.

She turned and looked at herself in the mirror. She did not ask why the women had wanted to disguise themselves: Julia wondered if she knew, or thought she did. She saw her daughter suddenly irradiated by the desire not to see or to know, but to take; to take life where the fine, feather-like divinations of her youthful instinct told her it lay.

'Very mysterious!' the woman cried out, laughing, as though she were not at all weary of people doing in her shop what Charlotte had just done.

Charlotte turned in her exotic, cruel plumage to her mother.

'Can I have it?'

'I don't think so,' Julia said, with a smiling roll of her eyes at the woman.

'Why not?'

'Because I don't think you would use it.'

'I would!'

'And because I've already bought *far* too many things,' Julia said, with another roll of her eyes.

Charlotte turned and regarded herself again in the mirror.

'Then I'll buy it myself,' she said, speaking to her reflection.

Julia did up her coat and went and looked at a display of masks nearer the door.

'Come on, darling,' she said. 'It's late. I'm sure the *signora* wants to close up her shop.'

The woman made a smiling gesture to the heavens, as

though it were not in her power to decide to want such a thing.

'I'll pay for it myself. You'll have to give me the money and I'll pay you back.'

'I don't have any money,' Julia replied benignly.

'You do!'

'I don't. It's all spent.'

'What about the money you were going to spend on dinner?' Charlotte said imperiously from behind her mask.

There was a pause.

'Let's go and talk about it,' said Julia meaningfully. 'We can always come back tomorrow.'

'Tomorrow, no,' interposed the woman. 'Tomorrow we are closed.'

'See? They're closed tomorrow. We have to do it *now*.'

The three of them looked at one another.

'Charlotte,' Julia said. 'I'm going.'

She put her hand on the brass door handle. The woman turned away and busied herself with something behind the counter. Julia opened the door and let in a stream of cold air, and when Charlotte did not come, as much out of consideration as anger, she let herself out of the shop and closed the door behind her. Standing in the little stone alley in the dark, she looked at the bright tableau of the shop window, with her daughter and the woman standing in it like two actors on a stage. Charlotte let the hand holding the mask slowly fall. With a downcast head she replaced it on the shelf. The woman was standing now with her arms folded, gazing obliquely at something through the window. She nodded as Charlotte passed her and through the glass Julia heard her say '*arrivederci*'.

'I'm sorry,' said Julia, who was not sorry at all, when Charlotte was outside.

'Just leave me alone,' Charlotte said, folding her arms and walking ahead.

Later, she *was* sorry: she found herself succumbing to the theory that the world was in fact a terrible and dangerous place, amidst whose manifold confusions she had thought to crush her daughter's tentative ideas of beauty. Shouldn't they all just cling together, and be as kind as they could? On the *vaporetto*, with Charlotte sullen and sighing on the seat beside her, she became aware of the scrutiny of a girl sitting opposite them, a girl in an immaculate white woollen coat and high-heeled boots whom Julia guessed to fall exactly between their ages, as though she were the missing part of their set and this might explain why she was looking at them so intently. She gazed at them with her large, clear eyes. Her plump, glossy lips were motionless. The more she stared the more Julia felt her perplexity. She seemed to find Julia and Charlotte inexplicably squalid. A thick, pale fog had suddenly descended over the canal, and through the window Julia saw the black beaks of the tethered gondolas rising and falling on the water in the gloom. Their agitation was disturbing: it was faintly lunatic, their interior rocking. The white air closed around them.

'You can choose what we do today,' Julia said the next morning – their last – at breakfast. 'The flight doesn't go until five. We'll do whatever you want.'

'OK,' Charlotte said. She seemed only slightly surprised. She straightened in her chair and looked around her with an aura of election.

'I've drunk so much water that I think I've washed away my soul,' Julia added.

'Is that a good thing?' Charlotte asked.

What Julia liked about children was the way they started where you left off, like runners waiting down the track with their hands outstretched for the baton. They took it – what was irreducible and final, what resisted all the sifting and the efforts to comprehend – and they ran; ran on lanky legs out of your failure or your contentment or your unwearying ambivalence and left you to unfold, to find your own level again.

Julia said: 'I think it definitely is.'

They found a painting in a church near Tintoretto's house, of the young Mary being presented at the temple. She was a little golden child, a girl, ascending a great rounded stone staircase in a pool of light. The broad, twisting women were here again: she had made her path through them where they sat or stood on the stairs. At the top a towering bearded man in clerical garb waited, dreadful, judging. The women turned and looked at her as she passed. They admired her and they were frightened for her. They were seeing something new.

TESSA HADLEY

Pretending

EVERY YEAR at our junior school the circus children
would appear for a few weeks. The school was at the
top of a steep Bristol hill of shops and houses; behind it the
Downs began, miles of open grass and woods across to
the steep gorge and the suspension bridge, where the river
crawled at the bottom in its shining mud. At the edge of the
Downs the circus tent was set up once a year, with behind
it a sprawl of caravans belonging to the circus performers,
and the trailers where the animals were kept. You could
pay extra money to go round after the circus show and see
the animals. My mother never wanted to, but once I
persuaded her, and then I regretted it because I hated
the way the men and women, changed out of their per-
forming clothes, came to the doors of the caravans and
watched us, saw my mother picking her way in the twi-
light, in her heels, across the churned muddy grass. I'd
imagined we could go on being invisible behind the scenes
as we had been in the audience. The man who showed us
round coaxed us, he sensed the danger that we'd be
disenchanted, he persuaded me to stroke the nose of
one of the white ponies. In his cage the lion reeked, his
coat was marked with scars like an old carpet, the contrast
of his shaggy heavy head with his slinking male hindquar-
ters made me uncomfortable. But I had so loved the

animals in the show, their happy teasing relationship with their masters.

When the circus arrived, the circus children all came to our school and were put on the register but most of them didn't seem to speak any English and didn't last long. For a day or two they sat sullen and dumb in the classroom and then electrified us in the playground with bowling cartwheels, walking on their hands, the lightning flares of their incomprehensible chatter and their fighting; after that half of them were never seen again. Or perhaps we saw them when we went to the circus and didn't recognise them in their unimaginable other lives, slinging ropes, taking money, fearless on the bare backs of the white ponies. We were glad and sorry that they didn't stay at school: they left behind in imagination a raw scorch of grace. Other circus children managed school better and did stay for a few weeks until the circus moved on. One of the girls I remember had long ringlets of chocolate brown hair tied up every morning in a white satin bow at the back of her head: this was the 1960s, so we mostly had our hair chopped off short, or in bunches. We fussed over her, making her folding fortune-tellers out of paper, teaching her our games, 'May I?' and 'Off-ground Touch', giving her our dolls to keep overnight. When she gave them back they smelled spicy and musty from wherever they'd been; some of the girls didn't like the smell, they wouldn't play with those dolls again, they said their mothers complained their bedrooms needed fumigating. The circus girl started off her new exercise books obediently, although she knew that she wouldn't be with us for long: pressing back the blue cover from the first page and ruling a margin in pencil, copying the date and the title in her foreign handwriting. She kept her accomplishments modestly to herself. When we begged her she would tuck the skirt of her dress into her knickers and skip upside down on to her hands, then bend backwards into what we called a crab, and then flip from there upright again, as fluently as if she was taking an ordinary step on her feet, shaking the dirt of our playground afterwards out of her curls.

My friend Roxanne wasn't from the circus, but somehow, perhaps because of how she looked, and because of her name too, she got muddled up with the circus children in my imagination, and when I think of her now I remember them. She was from the Homes. Roxanne chose me for her friend, I didn't choose her. She had always been on a different table, with the naughty girls: she had been one of the naughtiest. I don't think we'd ever even spoken, until on the day we began Junior Three she put her grubby furry pencil case on the desk beside mine and sat down there as calmly as if it had been prearranged between us. At first I thought it was a joke, which would end in my humiliation, so I wouldn't look at her. The teacher thought this too, she noticed us uneasily. We were new to her class, but it was a small school, the teachers knew all the children, they knew that girls like Roxanne weren't meant to be friendly with girls like me.

But Roxanne didn't get up to any of her usual tricks. When I put up my desk lid to put my new books inside the desk, she didn't knock it down on my head. Usually, when the teacher was talking, Roxanne twitched in her seat like a trapped cat, sitting on her hands to keep them from straying, her head twisting around to see what the boys were doing every time there was the sound of a scuffle or a muffled protest. Now she gazed at Mrs Hazlehurst, seeming to soak up every word she was saying. Mrs Hazlehurst was choosing the ink monitor and the milk monitor; she was telling us how hard we had to work, if we wanted to pass in two years' time the examinations for free places in the grammar schools. Roxanne volunteered for everything, holding her arm up straight above her head, tensed and still, although she wasn't chosen. When it came to playtime she gripped on to me as we filed down the corridor to go outside, not painfully but determinedly; she wasn't going to let me go. I was afraid of her and hot at the idea that the others were watching us. I had had a couple of friends in Junior Two and of course they would have expected us to go on sitting and playing together, although our friendship hadn't been passionate. As Roxanne marched me past them they seemed already faint and pale, as if they belonged to the weak past.

– What do you play? Roxanne demanded.
– I dunno. Whatever the others are playing.
– That's boring. Come on. We'll think of something else.

The boys' playground was on the left and the girls' on the right; they were deep concreted pits between very high stone walls. The girls' playground extended on one side into a covered area underneath the school building, supported on iron pillars; we called this the shed, and when it rained it was our shelter. Roxanne led the way in here, still hanging on to me, as if she was afraid I might run. It was an eerie echoing space, almost dark at its far end where the big bins were, and the padlocked grey-painted doors into the boiler room and the room where the caretaker kept the broken desks and blackboards. We sat down on the low wall in front of the bins. Everyone outside was still standing around in awkward groups, not sure how to begin yet in the new hierarchy, with a new top class and new Junior Ones arrived from the infant school.

Roxanne was inches shorter than me; I was tall, and clumsy with what my mother called puppy fat. I also had two big white front teeth like spades, which I had hated ever since they intruded their way into my mouth; I tried not to open it and show them. Roxanne's lithe little brown-skinned body made the boys call her a tomboy, although close up to her I realised that this wasn't right, she didn't have the boys' animal carelessness, she was too intently conscious of herself. Her red cotton dress was skimpy over her barrel chest, I could see her quick breathing. The skin of her face was very thin and fine, drawn tight over the bone beneath, and her head was round and neat as a nut: she was one of those children disconcertingly printed with a set of grown-up features, too finished and expressive. Her dark, silky, curly hair was cropped short. I used to imagine that if it had been allowed to grow long, it would have grown in ringlets like the circus girl's.

– What do you want to play? she said, turning on me with intensity. A pretending game. You can be whatever you like.

I shrugged.

– What do you like best? I'm good at making up these games. If you give me an idea, I'll make a game.

– Horses, I said, trying to think of something. I like horses.

I thought she was going to give up on me. I was a very conventional child, I knew I was. I saw a flicker of exasperation. Horses! Horses didn't mean anything to her. They didn't really mean much to me either; I had read some pony books, that was all. With an effort that was almost a visible shudder she pulled herself back on track.

– Horses, she said. All right. We'll try that.

She closed her eyes. The life of her eyes was extinguished for a moment but through their lids I could still see her thoughts darting. When she opened them again they were full of resolution.

– All right. Pretend we're horses. Wild ones. Take your hair band off. You have to shake your mane like this. There's a wicked farmer who's trying to catch us and sell us. We have to reach the island where we'll be safe from him, but there's a dangerous river we have to cross to get to it.

She jumped to her feet then and snickered and tossed her head and stamped her foot. She seemed to me miraculously horse-like. I took my hair band off and put it safe in my pocket, then we galloped around the playground, pawing and whinnying, throwing back our heads and shaking our hair; when we spoke we changed our ordinary voices into a kind of breathy neighing. At first I felt like an idiot and I only did it because I didn't dare disobey Roxanne, who had thought up the game especially for me. I saw my old friends watching, from the sidelines as usual. The others had started playing their own things, which some of the popular Junior Four girls were organising. These popular girls weren't used to the sight of Roxanne and me together; they stared and whispered, drooping their arms round one another's necks, which was a thing I hated. I thought they were like witches when they hung together like that, as if they only had one body, all thinking the same thoughts, always disapproving of something. A teacher had read us a story once about some old witches who shared one eye, taking turns to clap it into their foreheads.

After a few minutes of the horse game, I began to forget about everybody. I didn't exactly stop knowing that we were in the real playground, pretending something, but a different life welled up from inside me and took possession of my body, so that I could feel the romance of horse-being overwhelming my prosaic self.

– I don't think I can go any further, I neighed when we came to the edge of the river (which ran past the door to the girls' toilet block). I feel too weak.

– Fear not, young colt, said Roxanne.

She would always surprise me by knowing the right words for whatever we played, like using 'mane' and 'colt', even though she wasn't interested in horses. I had imagined that the children from the Homes, because they had to wear hand-me-down clothes and were looked after by women they called their 'Aunties', would be somehow deprived of these kinds of knowledge. Then she invented an extraordinary movement for horses swimming, holding back her head on her neck, making a nervous big digging movement with her hands, lifting her knees; and it was as if I could see them, the beautiful band of noble beasts giving themselves up courageously to the swift-flowing treacherous river, holding up their fine heads out of the current. After a hiatus mid-stream when I was in danger of being swept away, and Roxanne, swimming by my side, saved me, nudged me onwards with her nose, we both struggled out on the far bank, shaking ourselves dry, safe at last.

– See-ee-ee? she neighed. I knew you would be able to do it.

And then the teacher came out ringing the bell for the end of playtime.

Every morning when Roxanne came into the classroom I expected her to take her books out of the desk next to mine and move away to sit by someone else, giving no more explanation for leaving than she had when she'd first arrived. I half wanted her to go: our friendship burdened me, it was too one-sided, I never believed that she had really chosen me for what I was, I felt myself merely tumbled along in the wake of a change that she was arranging in her life. She had been one of the naughty girls and she had made up her mind quite deliberately to become one of the good girls; she saw me as a way of getting in to that. I never believed in those days that she would really make it as a good girl. There was too much of her: no matter how hard she tried she was bound to give herself away in the end, she would overdo it, they would see she was only pretending, that she wasn't the real thing. She concentrated on every-thing Mrs Hazlehurst said too intently, she put her hands together too fervently at prayers, raised them up too high in front of her face, eyes squeezed shut (mine weren't, that's how I saw her).

I could have ended our friendship any time I suppose; simply acted so dumb and resistant that Roxanne would have given up and fastened on to someone else. But I didn't. I couldn't help being swept along by the idea of someone changing who she was: I knew I wasn't capable of this, I was just helplessly for ever me. And then, I was soon addicted to the heady life of our pretend games. Perhaps it wasn't quite true that anybody would have done to be Roxanne's partner in these. What I learned, playing with her, was that I was suggestible, unusually suggestible. Later in life it turned out that I was a perfect subject for hypnotism: the hypnotist only had to wave his hand pretty much once across in front of my eyes and I was gone. I had never played proper pretend games before Roxanne started me off on it, except mothers and babies, half-heartedly, with my old friends, where the 'baby' hopped heavily along, crouched double, knees bent, holding hands with the 'mother' and saying 'ga-ga', which we knew babies didn't really say. We had only done it because everyone else did. When Roxanne and I played having babies it was very different. We did childbirth first, moaning and writhing against the iron pillars in the shed, throwing our heads from side to side and having our brows wiped (mostly I moaned, Roxanne wiped and presided). Then the imaginary babies were wrapped tenderly in our cardigans and carried about in our arms. We gazed into their tiny faces, we suckled them secretly in the dark corners of the shed, putting them to where we pretended we had breasts, though not lifting our jumpers of course. I don't know how Roxanne knew about childbirth or suckling; certainly I had only had the vaguest idea about either of them. When she came to my house and we played the game there, we did lift our jumpers up, we put my plastic dolls to our nipples on our flat chests. When I fed my own first real child I remembered this, the guilty delicious excitement of it, the sensation of pressing on those hard cold mouths.

My mother didn't like my friendship with Roxanne. She didn't mean to be unkind or prejudiced but she was afraid for me, she felt our mismatch, the inappropriateness of Roxanne's little skimpy gypsy body flashing enthusiastically up and down our familiar wood-panelled staircase, sitting before the hunting-scene placemat at our dining table, pouring from our gravy boat. When Roxanne used our bathroom she would never close the door, she had a funny habit of calling out to me all the time she was using it – 'Are you still there? Are you still there?' – so that I had to stay outside and hear her tinkling, scrunching the toilet paper. The smell she left behind her was alien. I knew that every time one of the Aunties turned up after tea to take Roxanne back to the Homes, my mother had to restrain herself from looking round to see if Roxanne had taken anything, which was awful and made us both ashamed. She also felt guilty that Daddy, who didn't like to get the car out, wouldn't give them a lift home, so that they had to wait for the bus. We lived across the Downs, in a street of trees and big detached houses with fake half-timbering, although I didn't know that it was fake then. When Roxanne was gone my mother would come and stand uneasily in the door of my bedroom, looking vaguely at my Wendy house, my dolls' cradle, the sewing basket given to me by my godmother, my set of red-bound classics: *Westward Ho!, The Cricket and the Hearth, Wuthering Heights, Cranford, East Lynne*. If I finished one of these classics my father gave me half a crown, so I ploughed through them one after another. If he questioned me about them I hardly knew what had happened in the one I had just finished, but he gave me the half crown anyway. Probably he had no memory of what had happened in them either, although he claimed that they were all old favourites from his childhood. Roxanne had snatched my books down eagerly when she first came to play, but even she found them too stodgy.

Instead she would sit cross-legged on my bed thinking up games. My younger sister was sometimes allowed to be part of this. I showed Roxanne off to Jean, as if I was showing off a forest wild animal I had tamed, but Jean was sceptical, she never refused to play but she turned her mouth down sullenly and acted as if her body was stiff, her spirit withdrawn from her performance. Roxanne made quite a show out of the difficulty of getting the right story. She sat with her eyes squeezed shut, and sometimes as if that darkness wasn't enough she asked for something to drape over her head: my dressing gown, or the coverlet off the dolls' cradle. Jean and I had to kneel still and quiet as mice on the bedside rug while Roxanne searched for inspiration. When she pulled her coverings away her eyes would be gleaming, full with her idea. It might be cruel governesses, or Mary

192

Queen of Scots, or pirates. There were games we played over and over, and games we only played once. Roxanne was always the men and we were the women, even though she was only the same size as Jean. I was often feverish or fainting or debilitated in some way, I kept in the cabin below (the bed), while Roxanne swaggered on the deck above (the floor), boldly fighting for our lives, her sword dangling at her side or slicing the air. We had to imagine that the cue from our miniature billiards was a sword, we didn't have dressing-up things. Jean and I had to wear our nightdresses, for old-fashioned-days clothes.

– Don't you have a dressing-up box? Roxanne was surprised, triumphant. We have them at the Homes.

What happened in our lives when we grew up, Roxanne's and mine, is not at all what I expected in those days. I expected Roxanne to be glamorously and terribly destroyed, and for me to survive safely and dully, achieving everything my parents expected of me. Then actually it was I who made a mess of growing up, although things have been better recently. I had a breakdown in my first year of university, and for a long time after that I couldn't work, I had to live back at home with my parents. I did get married but that didn't last, although at least I have my kids, who are grown up now. And the other day I heard of Roxanne, through someone I work with who'd been at school with her, not that junior school but her secondary one. I work in an insurance office, it's not very exciting but I can cope with it. I haven't seen Roxanne since we were about seventeen. Apparently these days she's an administrator in the Child Health Directorate in a big hospital in the north. The person who told me about her said she was 'a real high-flyer'. While he was telling me all this I did wonder whether we could really be talking about the same person; but surely with that name he couldn't have mixed her up with anybody else, he couldn't be mistaken.

I remember very exactly the last time I saw her. Roxanne and I went to different secondary schools. I did get into one of the grammar schools although I didn't get a free place; Roxanne was never even put in for the entrance exam, I don't think any of the children from the Homes were. For a while we saw each other sometimes at weekends; it was during this time, I think, that she invented our religious cult. We used to leave offerings at a particular rock in a little woody copse on the Downs, and prick our fingers to make marks on it with blood. The offerings only started with pennies and flowers, but by the end – after I had stopped seeing Roxanne – I was offering all kinds of stuff, not only silly amounts of money but quite precious things, my bronze medal from swimming, my dead grandmother's ring. When I went back to the rock the offerings had always gone, and although of course I knew really that someone had simply taken them, I couldn't be absolutely sure, and so I had to leave even more next time. I imagined the spirit of the rock as greedy, destructive, needing propitiating. I still can't walk near that place today, although my friends say that I ought to try. When I heard that Roxanne had got ill, that she was starving herself and only weighed six stone, I couldn't help thinking that this was something the rock had exacted from her. Anorexia was just starting to be talked about a lot. I knew she was taken into hospital, and then came out again, and was supposed to be better.

When I was seventeen I had almost forgotten all about her, or at least I had stopped expecting to bump into her wherever I went. I had a Saturday job in Blue, a jeans shop on Park Street, I couldn't quite believe my luck that I'd got to work with the girls in such a fashionable place. We painted our eyelids and outlined our eyes with kohl, we shook our long hair across our faces, we wore dangly Indian silver earrings; although actually my earrings were clip-ons, I hadn't had my ears pierced yet. My father put on a show of jocular astonishment whenever he met me at home dressed up to go out, claiming he didn't recognise me as his own daughter. The craze at that time was to buy jeans that fitted so tightly you had to do them up by lying on your back on the floor and pulling up the zip with string; I wasn't as pudgy as I had been once but I would rather have died than test myself doing this in front of the others. We went in fear of the full-time girls, who were disdainful, dangerous, enviably skinny. One had a boyfriend who rode a motor-bike and came into the shop in his fringed leather jacket. He touched her on the waist, and as they stood murmuring together we saw him nudge his knee between hers, hinting something, reminding her of something; she gave him money from the till. We knew that he sold drugs. All this was darkly intoxicating to us; these girls' lives seemed more truly adult to us than our parents' ever had.

One Saturday in Blue while I was folding a pile of cord trousers Roxanne came in at the shop door: I recognised her instantly although she was very changed. She looked im-pressive, she had exactly the air of initiated mysterious suffering that we were all aiming for. Her hair was hennaed a startling orange-red, not long but longer than I remem-bered ever seeing it, curling on her neck. Around her eyes and mouth her face was marked, as if it was bruised or strained; but this didn't make her ugly, it was somehow beautiful. She had grown into the painful expressivity of her features, which had been too much on a child. Her loose white cheesecloth dress was cinched around her tiny waist with a thick belt, pulling the cloth taut across her breasts, which weren't much bigger than when we'd fed our dolls together. Without looking at any of us she pulled a selection of size 8 jeans from the shelves and took them into one of the changing cubicles. I stood around wondering whether to say anything to her. I thought she hadn't recognised me, perhaps because she was high on something: her eyes were very wide open and she lifted her feet as if she was pulling them up from something sticky on the floor. Or perhaps she had just moved away into such a different life that she had blanked all memory of our friendship from her awareness.

After a long time she came out again from the cubicle, and it was obvious to me at once that she was wearing a couple of the pairs of jeans under her dress. She walked without any special haste straight to the shop door. Probably even if I hadn't known her I wouldn't have dared say anything: I was too shy to undergo the awful exposure of accusing anyone, incurring their contempt. Then as Roxanne walked out of the door she gave me one quick straight look, boldly into my face, and flashed her smile at me, like a flare of light illuminating the whole place, melting me. And I thought: I will always be the tame one, watching while she risks everything.

I believed then that this meant I would be safe, at least.

VICTORIA MARVIN

Honey Storms

T HE SKY turns lion-coloured and the wind gusts close to the ground. Honey seeps from every crevice. It happens every now and then, every four or five years I guess, during that curious time after the flush of summer has passed and before the crispy autumn begins. It is a meteorological phenomenon peculiar to our part of the world, I think, which happens for no apparent reason and leaves as quickly as it arrives.

They call it a honey storm, partly due to the honey colour of the atmosphere before the wind arrives, and partly because it causes bees to produce cloudy, tainted honey.

You can feel it coming, hours before it arrives, prickling at the base of your spine, powdery fingers tracing patterns on your skin, wings fluttering at your throat. Dust eddies into whirlwinds; the milk turns sour in the fridge. Horses bolt, dogs bark at the sky.

Most startling is the effect of the weather on people. Strange behaviour is observed, and no one is immune. Teenage girls in the full blush of vanity will hack off their hair at the skull. Good children set fire to their bedclothes. Marriage vows are made and broken, babies conceived, lives begun and ended. All within the space of a few stormy hours, in our silent, isolated bay.

*   *   *

My wife keeps bees. It's a common enough venture in this bay, where the manuka grows prolifically, hunched and close to the ground. Her hives are clustered at the far corner of our property, looking from the house like an impromptu meeting of stray washing machines.

I am violently allergic to bees.

The hives were purchased from our nearest neighbour, who had moved out of the area after his wife died. She fell, he said, and that was all he would ever say on the matter.

It's true that she fell; I saw it from our kitchen window. She fell from the apex of their two-storey house, landing crumpled and dead on the cement steps that lead up to their porch. I saw her climb out the upstairs bathroom window just as the sky began to take on its unnatural yellow tint. I watched as she balanced, one foot either side of the flashing, braced against the rising wind. I watched her for two and a half hours, looking out the window every now and then to see her waver precariously on her rooftop, buffeted by the wind and rain and hail of the honey storm. I saw her slip on the hot wet iron, lose her balance, windmill her arms and topple headfirst into space.

My own wife was not home during that honey storm, she had gone to the city for a day shopping and missed the whole event. I was alone in the house, voyeuristically watching my neighbour teeter on the roof for over two hours. I watched as her husband collapsed at her side, pulled her head into his lap, brushed her bloodied hair off her face.

And so he left, sold the house to a German couple and the hives to my wife. He moved the hives over on the back of his ute, deposited them in the corner of our property, and so began our lives of honey. My wife, at first, listened to my concerns about the bees. They could kill me, I reasoned, I could die. She removed any plants from the garden near the house which would attract them, sprayed pyrethrum on the door and window frames to repel them, had an insect screen installed on the sliding door. The fortress, she called it at first, as if the bees were her enemy as well as mine.

I was stung twice in the first summer, saved only by plunging the needle into my flesh before my body had time to react to the bees' poison. The first time, my wife drove me to the hospital, just to be safe. The second time, when I suggested this, she told me not to be so silly, and I knew that the bees were winning.

My wife took over the garden shed, relegated the lawnmower and garden tools to the space under the house, where they rusted in the damp. She whitewashed the walls of the ancient little shed and it became the honey house. It was there she bottled and stored her honey (until the shed was bulging with jars and she began to fill up the house), read books on bee keeping, blended and tasted the honey. She tasted and tasted the honey, at first tiny spoonfuls on the pretext of learning and improving her blend, and later, with a dessert spoon, spoon after spoon, half a jar at a time. I saw her once using her hand, scooping handfuls of honey from the jar into her mouth, frantically, it seemed, her arms and mouth smeared and sticky. When she saw me watching from the door of the honey house, she screamed at me, screeched. As I backed away, she threw a rolled-up copy of *The Bee Keepers Annual* at me, and I walked quickly back to the house.

I have been stung a number of times since that first summer, perhaps twenty. My wife says I must be building up a resistance to their venom by now. I say nothing. She does not get stung.

*   *   *

My wife is in the honey house, halfway between our house and the hives, when the sky yellows and the stickiness settles on my skin. My eyes grow hot and swollen, the backs of my hands itch and I have scratched them raw. I can feel the honey emanating from the pantry, borne on the very ether. The smell of it overwhelms me, I see it drip from the walls out of the corner of my eye. In the pantry, the shelves sag under the weight of the jars, row upon row of them, glowing the sickly colour of cats' eyes.

Outside, between our house and the honey house, where the lawn has been turned to dust by the scorching summer, a sinister wind sneaks along with its belly close to the hot ground. Anvil-shaped thunderheads are gathering behind the house, the colour of a five-day-old bruise.

As the wind picks up and storms through the open kitchen door, I hold a jar of honey in both hands. It breaks on the concrete floor between my feet, and the next one breaks beside it. The next one is smashed against the shelf, and I run the raw edge of the jar along my palm, gratified by the blood dripping off my elbow.

When all the jars are on the floor and there is blood and glass in the honey swirling around my ankles, my wife is standing at the door of the kitchen. Hailstones are making craters in the dust, and we are both wet with blood and honey and sweat. My wife looks me in the eye and, without turning her head, plucks a plate off the draining board. It sails slowly across the space between us and glances off my forehead. A pudding bowl hits my temple.

I move to her, my wife, my feet dragging through the sluggish honey. As I reach the door I am running, past her, across the yard, the hailstones slamming into my shoulders.

The wind trips me, blood runs down my arms and drips into the dust. I head for the hives.

The bees are agitated – I can hear them even before I reach the honey house. Rain and hail and dust and bees have filled the air; I push through them to the hives. By the time I have the lid off the first hive, my wife is running across the yard. I can hear her voice above the drone of the bees as I pull out the slides, as I am stung five times. Ten times. She reaches me as my tongue swells and my throat closes and I sink into the crisp yellow grass. As my eyes swell shut, she is screwing the syringe together with slippery hands.

I am helped up the stairs by my wife. She had dragged me by the ankles to the bottom of the porch steps, then lain beside me as the honey storm raged and my throat opened enough to let in a trickle of air.

Honey and blood and glass and china are settled on the kitchen floor. My wife and I sit together on the porch steps as the last of the yellow stain drains from the sky and we hold hands, the shard of glass still buried in my hand pressing into both of our palms.

About the Authors

After graduating in Classics from Oxford University, KATIE BARRON was a journalist on *Investors Chronicle* and the *Financial Times*. In 1996 she switched to teaching and has taught in London, Dublin and Trieste. While in Dublin her story 'Empath' was shortlisted for the Francis MacManus Award and broadcast on RTE One. Katie is now studying for an MA in Creative Writing at Bath Spa University. Her book on walking the pilgrim route to Santiago de Compostela can be found at www.peacepilgrim.freeuk.com.

ANNA BRITTEN is a freelance arts journalist living in Bath. After reading Modern Languages at Oxford she spent several years in London working for record companies, and then for *Time Out*, followed by a stint in Paris. She started writing short stories as a teenager, but has only recently started doing so again. She was also a prizewinner in the Frome Festival Short Story Competition.

MÁIRE COONEY was born in Edinburgh in 1970 and lives in London. She is working on a collection of short stories.

RACHEL CUSK was born in 1967 and is the author of the novels: *Saving Agnes*, winner of the Whitbread First Novel

Award, *The Temporary, The Country Life*, winner of a Somerset Maugham Award, *The Lucky Ones, In the Fold*, longlisted for the Man Booker Prize 2005, and *Arlington Park*, shortlisted for the Orange Prize 2007, plus a work of non-fiction: *A Life's Work: On Becoming a Mother*. In 2003, she was selected as one of Granta's Best of Young British Novelists.

PATRICIA DUNCKER is the author of four novels: *Hallucinating Foucault*, winner of the Dillons First Fiction Award and the McKitterick Prize; *James Miranda Barry*; *The Deadly Space Between*; and most recently *Miss Webster and Chérif*, shortlisted for the Commonwealth Writers' Prize 2007. She has also written two books of short stories, *Monsieur Shoushana's Lemon Trees* and *Seven Tales of Sex and Death*. She is Professor of Contemporary Literature at the University of Manchester.

BRENDA EISENBERG was a publishing director for an educational publisher until she did an MBA and started working as a freelance consultant. She now writes part time and is completing her first novel, *Ten Billion Square Feet of Perfection*. Her second novel is set in the orthodox Jewish community of South Africa during the apartheid era. She was born in South Africa and has lived in London for fifteen years.

MARIAN GARVEY lives in Brighton, has taught drama in schools, is a trained counsellor and holds an MA in Creative Writing from the University of Sussex. She is currently working on a collection of short stories, *Loss*.

TESSA HADLEY was born in Bristol and lives in Cardiff;

she is married and has three sons. She has published three novels: *Accidents in the Home*, *Everything Will Be All Right* and *The Master Bedroom*, plus *Sunstroke*, a collection of stories, and a book on Henry James. She teaches at Bath Spa University.

EMMA HENDERSON was born in London and lives there now, having recently returned from six years of living and working in France. She completed an MA in Creative Writing at Birkbeck in 2006, and is currently writing her first novel, *Grace Williams Says It Loud*.

JANEY HUBER is half Dutch and half Canadian, was brought up in Switzerland, and has lived in America, England and Oman. She has now settled in Cambridge and earns an income as a medical journalist. She is working on a novel about Geneva.

NANCY LEE lives in Vancouver, Canada. Hailed by the *Globe & Mail* as 'a masterwork of revelation', her collection of stories, *Dead Girls*, was published in Canada, the UK (Faber & Faber), France, Italy, Germany, the Netherlands and Spain. A recipient of the VanCity Book Prize, a National Magazine Award and a Gabriel Award for Radio, Nancy is currently working on a novel.

GABI MacEWAN has a grown-up son and currently lives in Devon. She knew she wanted to be a writer at the age of three (when her grandmother taught her to read) but her mind and hands have been distracted by many other occupations in the intervening years. Inspired by successes in recent competitions and the appreciation of friends, she is now working on a collection of short stories.

LOIS McEWAN is a freelance sub-editor working mainly for the *Sunday Times* and *The Times*. Her poetry has been published by Virago in the *New Poets* anthology, broadcast on ABC Radio in Australia and won an award in the Scottish International Poetry Competition. She is from Edinburgh and, after working on newspapers in Hong Kong and Australia, now lives in Westcliff with her husband and two sons.

VICTORIA MARVIN is a New Zealander working and travelling in the UK, Europe and Canada. 'Honey Storms' is her first finished story, and was inspired by the unpredictable weather and peculiar people of her home at the bottom of the world.

MIRIAM MOSS is a children's author of award-winning picture books and poetry. She is married with three children and lives in Sussex. 'Looking In' was her first short story. She is currently working on several new picture books and a collection of short stories. More information about her children's books can be seen at www.miriammoss.com.

EMILY PERKINS is the author of the story collection *Not Her Real Name* and the novels *Leave Before You Go* and *The New Girl*. Further short stories have been widely anthologised. Her new book, *Novel About My Wife*, will be published by Bloomsbury in 2008.

KATE PULLINGER's books include the novels *A Little Stranger, Weird Sister, The Last Time I Saw Jane* and *Where Does Kissing End?* and the short-story collections *My Life as a Girl in a Men's Prison* and *Tiny Lies*. Kate also writes for digital media; you can find her latest multi-media piece, *Inanimate Alice*, at www.katepullinger.com. She is Reader in Creative Writing and New Media at De Montfort University; she lives in London.

KATHRYN SIMMONDS was born in Hertfordshire in 1972 and now lives in north London. Her stories have appeared in magazines and been broadcast on Radio 4. She also writes poetry and her first collection will be published by Seren in 2008. Her favourite writers include Flannery O'Connor, Bob Dylan and Frank O'Hara.

A NOTE ON THE TYPE

The text of this book is set in Linotype Sabon, named after the type founder, Jacques Sabon. It was designed by Jan Tschichold and jointly developed by Linotype, Monotype and Stempel, in response to a need for a typeface to be available in identical form for mechanical hot metal composition and hand composition using foundry type.

Tschichold based his design for Sabon roman on a fount engraved by Garamond, and Sabon italic on a fount by Granjon. It was first used in 1966 and has proved an enduring modern classic.